When Last See My Mother?

A PLAY IN SIX SCENES

By Christopher Hampton

SAMUEL FRENCH, INC.
45 WEST 25TH STREET   NEW YORK 10010
7623 SUNSET BOULEVARD HOLLYWOOD 90046
LONDON   TORONTO

CHARACTERS

IAN

JIMMY

MRS. EVANS, *Jimmy's mother.*

DENNIS

LINDA

The first West End performance of WHEN DID YOU LAST SEE MY MOTHER? was given at the Comedy Theatre, Haymarket, London on July 4th, 1966. It was directed by Robert Kidd and the cast was as follows:

IAN	*Victor Henry*
JIMMY	*Julian Holloway*
MRS. EVANS	*Gwen Watford*
DENNIS	*Christopher Matthews*
LINDA	*Lucy Fleming*

When Did You
Last See My Mother?

HOSTILITIES COMMENCE

A faded but spacious bed-sit containing: two divans, one against the back wall, one against the side wall, a large, unwieldy table with ornamental legs, at the back with two or three chairs, a sofa with a holed red cover and one arm stove in, an armchair to match, a TV set set on a small round table, bookshelves, a telephone, a transistor radio, one chest of drawers decorated with an extremely scruffy, thin piece of green cloth, horrible pattern wallpaper, a gas fire, and various other odds and ends like raincoats hanging behind the door—all plonked down, it seems, on one huge all-purpose filthy red carpet. To add to the general air of constriction, the room is in an extremely untidy state, with books left about, dirty shirts on the chest of drawers. Occasional bottles, shoes and other bits and pieces litter the floor. The thick blue velvet curtains, souvenirs of another era, are pulled, and the two bottle lamps on the mantelpiece above the fire shed a dim light.

The two occupants of this room, IAN and JIMMY, are in the middle of a violent argument. JIMMY, fairhaired, handsome in a petulant sort of way, careful in his dress and hairstyle, stands, hands in pockets,

*facing one of the side walls, an expression of great
annoyance on his face. IAN is sitting glumly in the
big armchair. He is not good-looking—he wears
glasses, has a slight stoop, greasy, unmanageable
hair. He does not look angry, but cool, sardonic,
rather vicious. Both are in their very late teens.
They are, in fact, both rather drunk—IAN rather
more so than JIMMY, though they do not show any
conventional signs of this, such as slurring their
syllables or hiccuping or any of the usual unneces-
sary business of stage drunkenness. If it shows at
all it is in the thrusting belligerence of their talk.
After the curtain rises there is a short, poisonous
silence.*

IAN. (*Evenly.*) Crap. She was a right bag.

JIMMY. (*Bursts out.*) You are a . . .

IAN. She was a right soggy Weetabix. Don't tell me
you fancied her. You couldn't have. I know you're pretty
short on intelligence but I thought you had a modicum of
taste.

JIMMY. (*Explodes.*) Taste!?

IAN. The fifth and sixth sense.

JIMMY. Don't you talk to me about taste. Taste?
That's one thing you haven't got. I know for a fact my
taste is better than yours.

IAN. How?

JIMMY. Well . . . well, what about that god-awful
moo you knocked around with last year—Hilary or
Amelia or whatever her name was?

IAN. Carol.

JIMMY. Yes—well, she looked like a tin can in labor.

IAN. You never even met her.

JIMMY. She must have done if she went to bed with
you. Anyone who did, would.

IAN. (*Stung by this, gets up.*) —Aren't you being
rather childish? Anyhow she didn't. Look like that or go
to bed with me.

Jimmy. So are you.

Ian. So am I what?

Jimmy. Oh, belt up!

(*Silence. For a moment it seems as if the argument has come to an end. Then* Jimmy *kicks a shoe across the room.*)

Ian. Oh, you are a scruff. (*He turns to* Jimmy, *annoyed.*) She was, though.

Jimmy. What?

Ian. A bag. Horrible. I could tell her a mile off. The way she came up. (*He imitates her, a simpering falsetto.*) "What's your name? Jimmy what? Oo, I've heard about you." And then you went all pathetic and asked her what she'd heard, and when she said, "Aha," I nearly retched it was so inevitable. It was quite obvious she'd never heard of you before either.

Jimmy. (*Rather miserably.*) She had.

Ian. Like hell. (*Pause.*) Mind you, it wasn't so much your degrading yourself with a third-class tart that annoyed me, it was making we wait an hour after everyone else had gone home while you filled her in in her car. That was not only boring but embarrassing. By the time you turned up the host was getting quite nasty.

Jimmy. Oh, don't keep on, for Christ's sake.

Ian. Well, it was a terrible party.

Jimmy. Well, you don't seem to go out of your way to enjoy yourself.

Ian. That's because the only decent birds are already booked and only the ugly, sex-starved crows like you got are left.

Jimmy. She wasn't ugly.

Ian. She had a reasonable pair of Bristols, I remember noticing. But her face was dull, Christ, and listening to her yattering must have been like walking on red-hot coals.

Jimmy. So you just resign and drink.

IAN. Yeah, that's right. And ogle the few respectable birds like that one in trousers and boots.

JIMMY. That was the host.

IAN. (*With a sudden outbreak of viciousness.*) Look, why don't you shut up and before you start making snide remarks, just remember yourself at school, last year.

JIMMY. (*Mumbles tiredly.*) Oh, bugger off.

IAN. (*Regaining his composure.*) I beg your pardon?

JIMMY. (*In a sudden blaze of fury.*) Bugger off!

IAN. For Christ's sake, keep your voice down or that Wop get will call the police again. If we have the police round more than once a week, dear, the neighbors will start talking. (*Suddenly* JIMMY *steps across and lashes out at* IAN, *who is genuinely surprised at this. He ducks out of the way.*) That was a joke. What I just said. A joke. Ha, ha? You thick turnip. You have a positive genius for missing the point. (*Pause—then, aggrieved.*) You want to watch what you're doing, you might have done me an injury.

JIMMY. (*Miserably.*) You are a bastard.

(*Silence. Their eyes meet for a second; then they both look away.*)

IAN. That's as may be. (*Pause. He looks at his watch.*) Christ, it's twenty to four. Bedtime, my lad. We got that job starting tomorrow morning, remember? (*Flops down on one of the beds and then, noticing that* JIMMY *has not answered and is in fact looking rather guilty:*) You do remember?

JIMMY. Well, yes, as a matter of fact, Ian, I wanted to tell you something about that.

IAN. (*Sits up, immediately suspicious.*) What?

JIMMY. Well, I . . . I've decided I don't want to do it. I don't fancy it.

IAN. You what?

JIMMY. Oh, God, I knew you were going to make a fuss about it. I wasn't going to tell you till the morning.

IAN. What do you mean you weren't going to tell me

till the morning? What do you mean (*His indignation is mounting.*) you knew I was going to make a fuss about it?

JIMMY. What I say.

IAN. What you say?

JIMMY. (*Becoming annoyed himself.*) Look, don't just stand there or . . . or sit there bloody well repeating everything I say. You heard.

IAN. Well, I don't think I get what you're on about.

JIMMY. Don't be so damn silly, of course you do. I am simply not going to come with you on the job tomorrow.

IAN. (*Flabbergasted.*) But I . . . you . . . we already signed on and everything.

JIMMY. Well, I've changed my mind. Look, let's face it, it's not really me lumping great loads of bricks around the place, now is it?

IAN. (*Has got to his feet. He is almost beside himself.*) But it was your lousy idea!

JIMMY. Yeah, and I still reckon it was a good one. Building sites is a good way to make money when you're down. But I've decided I don't want to do it and that's it.

IAN. But it was going to be all happy comrades. You said, you said all along that it wouldn't be too bad doing a laborer's job if we did it together. You said it would be—fun.

JIMMY. Well . . . I . . .

IAN. Of course, I never really expected you to soil your lilybloodywhite hands with honest toil. (*The quiet venom is back in his voice now.*) It's as much as you can do to write all those bloody letters home asking for more money. You nearly rupture yourself carrying all those pound notes around in your wallet.

JIMMY. Oh, don't start that again, for Christ's sake.

IAN. I'm surprised you deign to rub shoulders with an underprivileged pauper like me. Why don't you go and live with someone rich so that you can co-exist in the style to which you are accustomed? Like that collapsible haggis you were with this evening. You could sleep with her as well. (*An afterthought.*) Of course, you could always sleep with me, but Mummy wouldn't like that, would she?

JIMMY. (*Reasonably.*) I think you're bloody tactless, Ian. If I moved out you know very well you wouldn't be able to afford the rent.

IAN. Tactless? Yes, I am tactless. I come from a tactless family. Take my father. He was a very tactless man: (a) because instead of having me educated on the house he nearly broke himself giving me the inestimable benefits of a public school education, and (b) because he went and caught nasty, rotten, lumpy cancer and, tactlessly, as ever, timed his death for my sixteenth birthday. My mother was also tactless enough to die, when I was twelve.

JIMMY. Oh, spare us the poor orphaned me spiel for Christ's sake.

IAN. (*Is furious that his bubble of indulgent self-pity has been burst; he shrivels back into cold, probing anger.*) You were threatening me just now, weren't you?

JIMMY. (*Taken off guard.*) When? How?

IAN. You said it was tactless to annoy you because if you moved out I couldn't manage the rent.

JIMMY. Yes, well . . . I . . .

IAN. (*Erupts again.*) Well, I can do without you, see? You and your bloody money, flashing it round like you were the Sheik of Kuwait. There's other people in London who want to share a flat and who could do it without making out they were Aristotle Onassis.

JIMMY. Who?

IAN. (*With insulting relish.*) Aristotle Onassis.

JIMMY. Well, if that's the way you feel . . .

IAN. Yes, it is. You're damn tooting right, it is.

JIMMY. Look, I'm buggered if I'm going to stand here and listen to you griping all day and every day. You seem to forget I live here from choice, not because I have to. *I've* got a home to go back to, and . . . and (*He*

blusters, realizing suddenly the cruelty of his words.) I'm
bloody well going back to it.

IAN. Oh, why don't you. I can't imagine why you ever
came in the first place. (*Now he is hurt, shouting.*) Go
on, get packed and get out.

JIMMY. I will. (*Pause.*) I will. (*Crosses to the chest of
drawers and pulls out an immense old holdall from behind it. He opens one of the drawers and begins bundling
the contents into the holdall. IAN watches him silently
and malevolently. After a short time JIMMY pauses and
then strides over to the door.*)

IAN. Where are you off to now?

JIMMY. (*Coldly.*) I'm going to have a slash. Do you
mind?

IAN. Not in the least, my dear. Make yourself at home.
(JIMMY *stalks out, slamming the door. A pause, then*
IAN *begins to laugh quietly. Then he gets up, goes over
to the chest of drawers, reopens the drawer, takes*
JIMMY'S *clothes out of the holdall and puts them back in
the drawer. He closes the drawer, picks up the holdall
and drops it back down behind the chest of drawers. As
he has been doing this, he has been singing rather tune-
lessly in a heavy American accent:*)

>There is a house in Noo Orleans
>They call the Risin' Sun,
>An' it's been the ruin of many a po' boy,
>An', God, Ah know, Ah'm one.

(*Re-enter* JIMMY. *He goes across and looks for his
holdall, then turns wrathfully on* IAN *who is by now sitting in the armchair again.*)

JIMMY. You. . . . what? . . . (*He breaks off as he
sees* IAN *smiling at him.*)

IAN. My dear Jimmy, four o'clock in the morning is
hardly the moment to stage a dramatic walkout. I imagine one would feel a proper nig-nog storming out and
then having to wait two or three hours in a station waiting room full of snoring tramps.

JIMMY. (*Again uncertain.*) Yeah . . . well, let's have a bit less of this patronizing "my dear Jimmy" bit.

IAN. A thousand pardons, James, my heart's desire. That scans.

JIMMY. (*Suddenly smiling, almost affectionate.*) You are a sod.

IAN. You tell me that so often I'm beginning to believe you. No, but seriously, Jim, in all . . . seriousness, you must stop starting all these arguments.

JIMMY. (*Again enraged.*) Me? You . . . I . . . (*He breaks off as he hears* IAN *laughing low in his throat. Then he smiles and shakes his head.*) No . . . but listen, Ian, let me tell you something seriously—and this is serious—well, seriously, Ian, you shouldn't drink so much.

IAN. (*Mock concern.*) Are you serious?

JIMMY. (*Missing the sarcasm.*) Yes. Yes, I am. Because I tell you, you're a real bastard when you're drunk. Because . . . you lose control of your tongue . . . and you're bloody vindictive.

IAN. Thank you, Mrs. Dale.

JIMMY. Yeah . . . well, just you try and remember that.

IAN. Oh, I will. Yes. (*Pause. Then* IAN *gets up.*) Well now, much as I love you, I can't sit around chatting you up all night. Some people have to work to earn a living.

(*Silence.* IAN *walks across to his bed and begins to take off his sweater.*)

JIMMY. Listen, I've been thinking. . . .

IAN. (*Engulfed in sweater.*) Never.

JIMMY. Perhaps I will come with you on that job tomorrow.

IAN. You what?

JIMMY. I changed my mind.

IAN. Again?

JIMMY. Yes. (*He is beginning to get annoyed.*) Yes. I think I do need the money.

IAN. Oh, no.

JIMMY. No, what? What do you mean?

IAN. I'm not having you trailing along looking martyred. I'm not going to listen to you griping all day and blaming it on me. Oh, no.

JIMMY. Listen, you can't stop me if I want to work. We signed on for that job together . . . remember?

IAN. And then you decided you didn't want to go.

JIMMY. (*Bellows.*) Well, I've changed my mind!

IAN. Well, I'm perfectly capable of doing a job like that without you breathing down my bloody neck all day.

JIMMY. (*Still shouting.*) All right then, I won't go!

(*Long silence. IAN starts unbuttoning his shirt. Then he stops and fishes his wallet out of his back pocket. He inspects the contents and then puts it back.*)

IAN. Two pound ten. . . . I don't think I will either.

BLACKOUT

SCENE 2

TEA FOR THREE

A few days later. The room looks a little tidier and IAN *and* JIMMY *are in the process of clearing up.* IAN *is armed with a duster which he flicks carelessly over the furniture.* JIMMY *is picking up various bits and pieces and stuffing them into drawers. Their conversation is sporadic, interrupted by the actions of last-minute tidying-up.* IAN *stops dusting for a minute and looks nostalgic. He shakes his head and sighs quietly.*

IAN. He was beautiful. (*Silence.*)

JIMMY. (*Indifferently.*) He was all right.

IAN. It annoys me when you say things like that. Just offhand: "He was all right," just like that. After all, you did go to bed with him.

JIMMY. (*Does not answer for a moment. It seems he does not like being reminded. Finally he speaks.*) So what? Only because there was no one else going.

IAN. (*Stops dusting.*) Now that really does annoy me.

JIMMY. Why?

IAN. Because I was in love with him. I was in love with him and hardly ever spoke to him. You went to bed with him because there was no one else going.

JIMMY. As far as I can see you've only got yourself to blame. You should have told him. He'd have had them off like a shot. I've told you before, he was a pretty easy lay.

IAN. I . . . I was scared of him.

JIMMY. (*Amused.*) Why?

IAN. (*Fiercely.*) Because I was in love with him. (*Silence.* IAN *stands holding the duster, looking miserable.*)

JIMMY. Listen, are you going to dust or shall I? She'll be here in a minute.

IAN. What? Oh . . . oh, yes. (*Continues dusting for*

14

a minute then stops, suddenly struck by a thought.) You remember that last night?

JIMMY. No, what last night? When?

IAN. The last night of our last term.

JIMMY. No, not particularly.

IAN. I'm not surprised, you were stoned. (*Silence; IAN flicks aimlessly at the T.V. set.*)

JIMMY. Well, what about it?

IAN. What about what?

JIMMY. The last night.

IAN. Oh, nothing.

JIMMY. No, go on. You were going to say something about it.

IAN. No, I was just thinking about you on that last night.

JIMMY. Well?

IAN. Well, you were so drunk—you'd been mixing drinks all evening and you were really merry. You kept saying that you had a farewell appointment with Dennis at eleven o'clock and it was going to be the greatest.

JIMMY. And?

IAN. And then about eleven you got up and staggered off full of the sly winks and heavy nudges. And you were gone about an hour, maybe more, and I waited in my study till you came back to tell me how marvelous it had been, how fabulous he was, and I just sat there and listened to you babbling on and I thought what a way to end a school career and I thought you bastard because you knew.

JIMMY. (*A little worried.*) I don't remember all this.

IAN. I told you, you were pissed. As a cist. But I wasn't. (*Silence. He stands, remembering.*)

JIMMY. (*Deprecatingly.*) Well, anyhow, he wasn't all that marvelous.

IAN. (*Implacably.*) I thought so.

JIMMY. No, I tell you, he . . . er . . .

IAN. He what?

JIMMY. He had a . . . er . . . an anatomical deficiency.

IAN. A what?

JIMMY. An anatomical deficiency.

IAN. I'm not with you.

JIMMY. Well, work it out. (IAN *remains puzzled.*) Look, it's past four o'clock. For Christ's sake get a move on with that bloody dusting. (IAN *does not move.*) Look, are you or are you not going to dust?

IAN. (*Sepulchrally.*) We all are. (*He looks up at* JIMMY *smiling and* JIMMY *laughs, as the bell rings.* IAN *goes berserk.*) Oh shit, here she is. (*He rushes round the stage dusting everything in sight, including* JIMMY. JIMMY *laughs and takes the duster from him. While* JIMMY *is offstage,* IAN *straightens a few cushions and flops into the armchair. Just as he does so the door opens and* JIMMY *shows his mother in.* IAN *stands up.* MRS. EVANS *is a still attractive woman of about 40. She shares* JIMMY'S *fair hair and good looks and has not lost her figure. She is dressed smartly but tastefully. It is fairly obvious from her clothes, accent and bearing that she comes from a prosperous family, although prosperity does not seem to have spoilt her in any way.*) Hello, Mrs. Evans.

MRS. EVANS. Hello, Ian, nice to see you again. How are you?

IAN. Oh, you know, surviving.

JIMMY. Sit down, Mum. I'll go and get a cup of tea ready and you can have a chat with Ian.

MRS. EVANS. Thank you, dear. (*Sits down at one end of the sofa.* JIMMY *starts to leave the room.*)

IAN. I'll get it.

JIMMY. No, you sit down. I won't be long.

IAN. O.K. (*Sits down again in the armchair. There is a short silence. Then they both begin talking at once.*) Don't lean on the . . .

MRS. EVANS. You seem to have got . . .

IAN. Sorry.

MRS. EVANS. No, do go on.

IAN. I was just going to say don't lean on that arm of

the sofa. It's extremely collapsible. Now what were you going to say?

Mrs. Evans. I was going to say that you seem to have got Jimmy nicely house-trained. He'd never have dreamed of getting the tea before he left home.

Ian. Actually, he's much better at that sort of thing than I am.

Mrs. Evans. Really?

Ian. Yeah, I'm hopeless.

Mrs. Evans. And yet you've led a much more sort of . . . independent life than he has, haven't you?

Ian. I suppose so, yes.

Mrs. Evans. I mean, I suppose I shouldn't say a thing like this, but you always seem to be so much more mature than Jimmy.

Ian. (*After a short pause, smiling.*) Maybe that's why I'm so lousy at housework. (*Silence.*)

Mrs. Evans. (*Thoughtlessly.*) How are the family?

Ian. (*Smiling, offhand.*) Dead, mostly.

Mrs. Evans. (*Is covered with confusion at this. She blushes deeply and stammers when she speaks next.*) Oh, I'm terribly sorry . . . I . . . didn't mean . . . I meant your grandparents. I'm awfully . . . I mean . . . how . . .

Ian. Don't worry. I don't mind a bit. Really.

Mrs. Evans. No, honestly, it was frightfully thoughtless of me.

Ian. (*Kindly.*) Nonsense. (*Pause. He smiles at her.*) My grandparents are fine. They're still strongly opposed to my living here and want me to go back to Sheffield. But, God, it's such a dreary place—I'd far rather live here with Jimmy.

Mrs. Evans. It's expensive here, though, isn't it?

Ian. Ah, now, there you've touched upon a very delicate point. As a matter of fact my money from all those different jobs I did at the beginning of the year when I was staying with you has almost gone. The Paris holiday took up quite a bit of it and this place has eaten up the rest. Jimmy and I did have a job scheduled to start last week but there was a party on the Sunday night and on Monday we both had hangovers. I was sick all morning.

MRS. EVANS. But you've only got a couple of months before you go up to Oxford, haven't you?

IAN. Yes, but I would be hard pushed to exist for two months on my present capital, which amounts to 17/4d.

MRS. EVANS. (*Appalled.*) Is that all? Is that really all? (IAN *nods, smiling. Silence.*) Ian?

IAN. Mm?

MRS. EVANS. Look, if we could lend you some . . . you know, just twenty pounds or something . . . don't hesitate.

IAN. (*Smiling, shaking his head.*) No, I couldn't.

MRS. EVANS. Yes, I mean, just a loan. . . .

IAN. No, I wouldn't want to. Thanks a lot, it's very kind of you and all, but . . .

MRS. EVANS. Well, how are you going to manage?

IAN. I'll be O.K. As a matter of fact I'm signed on with an agency and they're going to ring me whenever they have a job going, which should be any day now, and I'll be able to start on Monday with any luck. We've got the weekend shopping in and the rent's up to date, so I shouldn't have to spend any more dough until Monday and I'll ask them to pay me in advance.

MRS. EVANS. What if they won't?

IAN. I'll manage.

MRS. EVANS. What if they can't give you a job?

IAN. I'll make out. (*Hastily changing the subject.*) Where's Jimmy gone with the tea then? (*Forced laughter.*) He's probably gassed himself or something. I'll go and see. (*Gets up and goes across to the door.*)

MRS. EVANS. Ian . . .

IAN. (*Smiling.*) You didn't hear an explosion, did you?

MRS. EVANS. No, I . . . (IAN *has left the room.*)

IAN. (*Offstage.*) Is it nearly ready? Can I fetch or carry?

Jimmy. (*Offstage.*) Get the table out, will you? (*Re-enter* Ian.)

Ian. Won't be a minute.

Mrs. Evans. (*Laughs.* Ian *comes across and sits.*) You've done something different to your hair.

Ian. Combed it.

(*They both laugh. Then* Jimmy *enters backwards with a tray of tea, cake, toast, etc. He sets it on the ornamental-belegged table.*)

Jimmy. (*A little self-consciously.*) Voilà. Shall I dispense?

Ian. Not in here, please.

Jimmy. (*Matily.*) Shut your face.

Ian. (*Walks over to the table and looks at the tea.*) Your usual valiant, if mediocre, effort. Dispense by all means and let's get it over with.

Jimmy. Look, let's have a bit less of the sparkling repartee. Entertain Mum while I hand round. Give her one of your stories.

Mrs. Evans. One of his whats?

Jimmy. Stories.

Ian. No.

Mrs. Evans. Oh, do. Go on.

Ian. No, not in the mood. (*Pause.*) Oh, all right then. (*Pause.*) Well now, this is a true and very tragic story, so no giggling, James.

Jimmy. I've heard it.

Ian. How do you know? Anyhow, as you so elegantly put it, shut your face. (Jimmy *discreetly dispenses as* Ian *speaks, and they eat and drink as they speak and listen.*) It was when I was in Paris earlier this year.

Jimmy. I have heard it.

Ian. Look, for . . . Please. (*Pause; they laugh.* Ian *continues.*) In Paris, anyway. I went to this Sorbonne lecture and it was this old girl lecturing on modern art and sculpture. Middle-aged she was, actually, and a bit or a droner. She gave a short address and then switched all the lights off and started showing slides of all these crummy modern sculptures, you know, with holes and all. Anyhow, she hadn't been going long before people started slipping out. Every now and then, you'd hear the swing-doors going as someone else left. Anyhow, she droned on and people kept going and going and she put more slides in and the swing-doors swung more and more often and finally—because I was accustomed to the dark by then—I looked around the hall and I was the only person left in the entire room. So I thought, Christ, this is going to be so embarrassing when the lights go on, we'll be alone, and she may even speak to me or something and my French is terrible, especially in times of stress, so I—quietly and guiltily—I crept out through the swing-doors. (*Pause.*) You can just imagine her at the end saying; "Thank you all for coming and listening and I hope you've all learnt something, all of you," and then switching the lights on and no one there.

MRS. EVANS. You should have stayed. You ought to have stayed.

JIMMY. (*Pensively.*) Poor old moo.

(*Slight silence.* IAN *turns to* JIMMY.)

IAN. I sit here; I tell a story so moving in its details and so deep in its implications, that the most hardened listener should melt into helpless tears. So Evans here, a . . . quagmire of hypersensitivity, is moved to comment in his own . . . inimitably colloquial way— Poor old moo. Poor old moo—the remark of a true aesthete.

JIMMY. (*Rolling his eyes.*) God alive.

MRS. EVANS. Well, really, Jimmy, he's right.

JIMMY. (*Harshly to his mother.*) Ian is being funny. You're supposed to laugh, not agree.

MRS. EVANS. (*Unhappily.*) Well . . .

IAN. There is, nevertheless, a groatsworth of truth behind my wit.

JIMMY. (*Suddenly blurting.*) You're a bit bloody pompous this afternoon, aren't you?

(*There is an awkward silence. IAN is silent because he knows JIMMY is right; MRS. EVANS because she is a little uncertain how to react; JIMMY because he wishes he had not spoken.*)

MRS. EVANS. Er . . . more tea? (*IAN disregards her question; he is brooding.*)

JIMMY. Yes, please.

MRS. EVANS. (*Sharply.*) I was asking Ian. (*Then immediately:*) Oh, I'm sorry, dear. Sorry I was a bit. . . . We're all . . .

IAN. (*Smiling suddenly.*) Yes. (*Pause.*) My fault. (*Silence. MRS. EVANS pours tea for JIMMY.*)

JIMMY. Thanks.

MRS. EVANS. (*At the same time.*) Ian?

IAN. Yes, thank you.

MRS. EVANS. (*Silence again. MRS. EVANS goes to pour IAN another cup but the tea runs out.*) None left. I'll have to go and fill it from the kettle.

JIMMY. (*Slightly embarrassed.*) I'll go.

MRS. EVANS. (*Already on her feet.*) You sit down. I'll deal with it.

IAN. Don't bother. I'm not all that keen for another cup.

MRS. EVANS. (*With finality.*) Won't take a minute. (*Exits with teapot. Short silence, then IAN catches JIMMY's eye and smiles at him.*)

IAN. Not going too badly, is it?

JIMMY. No, except . . . sorry I snapped.

IAN. Like I said, my fault. (*Silence.*)

JIMMY. She likes you a lot, you know.

IAN. Does she?

JIMMY. Yes, she's always saying.

IAN. Well, I like her. (*Silence.*) Jimmy.

JIMMY. Yeah.

IAN. Can you lend me a couple of notes?

JIMMY. (*The slightest hesitation.*) Sure, sure. (*Reaches for his wallet.*)

IAN. Not right now. After will do. That'll make it I owe you three quid. I should be able to pay you back fairly shortly.

JIMMY. (*A little hurt.*) Look, I told you I didn't need that other pound back.

IAN. Oh, God, don't let's go through all this again. You lend me a pound, I owe you a pound. I don't want bloody charity.

JIMMY. (*A little huffily.*) All right then, I won't lend you any more.

IAN. (*Stares at him poisonously for a moment; then, hissing.*) All right then, don't.

(*Re-enter* MRS. EVANS *with the teapot. She goes across to pour out some tea for* IAN.)

MRS. EVANS. Oh dear, it's very weak, I should have left it . . . (*She realizes suddenly that there is tension in the air.*) to stand.

IAN. (*An obvious effort.*) No, no, that's fine. I . . . er, don't mind it weak.

JIMMY. (*Also forced.*) Did I tell you, Mum, to change the . . . er . . . subject, that we're having a party here next Friday?

MRS. EVANS. Really. No, you didn't. A big one?

JIMMY. Just a few friends.

MRS. EVANS. From school?

IAN. Some.

MRS. EVANS. Oh, who's from school?

JIMMY. There's . . .

IAN. (*Slightly maliciously.*) Dennis. (*Short silence.*)

Mrs. Evans. Who's he?

Jimmy. (*A little strained.*) You don't know him. You don't know any of them.

Mrs. Evans. Oh. (*Pause.*) Sounds rather exciting. Can I come? (*She laughs.*)

Ian. (*Quickly.*) Would you like to?

Mrs. Evans. Mm. (*Smiling.*) I would, rather.

Jimmy. (*Sharply.*) Out of the question.

Mrs. Evans. Why? I mean I wouldn't dream of coming really, but why do you sound so horrified? (*She smiles.*) Do you have orgies or something?

Jimmy. Oh, Mother, don't be ridiculous.

Ian. Jimmy, you're a misery. Your mother would be the life and soul. She'd lend an air of tone to any . . . debauch that might occur. (*Smiles broadly at* Mrs. Evans.)

Mrs. Evans. (*Uncertain giggle.*) No, really, I've always wanted to be present at one of Jim's parties just to see what really happened.

Ian. You'd be bored stiff. It's just pop music and a lot of youths snogging. (*Hastily.*) And girls. Youths and girls.

Mrs. Evans. Sounds deadly.

Jimmy. It makes a change.

Ian. Rather a costly change, I may add. Still, with any luck next Friday will be my first payday. (*He sighs pleasurably.*) O.K., it's me for the washing up.

Mrs. Evans and Jimmy. (*Together.*) No, I'll do it. I'll go. (*Short silence.*)

Mrs. Evans. Let's all go and do it together.

Ian. Good idea. (Mrs. Evans *picks up the tray and heads for the door, which* Jimmy *opens for her.* Ian *goes to follow her but* Jimmy *stops him.* Jimmy *fetches out his wallet, takes out two pounds, crinkles them at* Ian *and hands them to him.* Ian *stuffs them into a pocket and smiles at* Jimmy. *He nods at him. He stretches out his hand and pats* Jimmy's *cheek.* Jimmy *looks faintly embarrassed but returns* IAN'S *smile. They hold each other's eyes for a moment.*) Thank you, darling.

(*They exit: as they do so . . .*)

BLACKOUT

AFTER THE PARTY'S OVER . . .

*About a week later. It is the small hours and the party
has almost broken up. There are empty bottles,
glasses and cigarette ends everywhere, and the room
is a shambles. All but two of the guests have left
and* JIMMY *can be heard offstage saying good-bye
to some of them. The two remaining guests are*
LINDA, JIMMY's *latest flame, a good-looking enough
girl, blond with trim figure, daddy-sent-me-to-art-
school-isn't-it-fun type, and* DENNIS, *a very good-
looking boy of about 16 or 17 who is slow of speech,
superficially, one would say, because he is slow of
wit.* IAN *is fairly drunk and is swigging red wine
from a one-half pint mug. He is sitting on the floor
against the armchair,* LINDA *is sitting on the sofa
and* DENNIS *is half-sitting, half-lying on one of the
beds, his feet not quite touching the floor.*

IAN. And so she said: (*Grotesque mincing imitation.*)
"I don't think you've put enough milk in it," or something, anyhow she griped and I . . . (*Takes a swig of
the wine, grimaces.*) Christ, this is foul.

DENNIS. Why drink it?

IAN. (*Disregarding the question.*) And so anyhow I
said, "Well, if you don't like it you can bloody well make
it yourself. . . ." (*During his speech* JIMMY *has entered.*)

JIMMY. Oh God, you're not telling this one again, are
you?

IAN. (*Doggedly.*) . . . or words to that effect and so
anyhow I was fired.

JIMMY. (*To* LINDA, *smiling.*) In a minute he's going to
tell you that he isn't cut out to be a bloody office boy.

IAN. (*Playing up.*) Anyhow I don't think I was cut out to be a bloody office boy.

JIMMY. We've all heard about it already.

IAN. Balls. They haven't. Have you?

LINDA. As a matter of fact I think I have. (*She giggles.*)

IAN. Tell us about Art School then.

LINDA. (*Uncertain.*) Well . . . I . . .

IAN. Never mind, I've got a better idea. I think I'll sing you a little song. Like that, Dennis?

DENNIS. Well . . . I . . .

IAN. Right, then. Here we go. A little song entitled, (*Sings.*) "Don't be afraid to sleep with your mother, just because she's older than you." No, actually, the song is really called "Oedipus' Lament at Colonnos." (IAN *sings viciously, filled with the acrid knowledge that he is embarrassing the others more than amusing them.*)

When I was sixteen, I fell in love
With a slightly older bird,
But I remembered what the prophet said
And those wise words I had heard.
'Cos he said,
Son, you are a bachelor boy
And that's the way to stay, hey hey,
Happy to be a bachelor boy
Until your dying day.
(*Pause.*) Verse Two, you unlucky people.

Then a bit later I fell once more
For another older dame, pom, pom,
I still remembered what the prophet said
But I married her just the same,
But I wish that
I'd stayed a bachelor boy
'Cos, though this is a welf-
Are state, it is bleedin' impossible to get
New eyes on the nashnal helf. Olé.

(*He grins tiredly and empties his mug of wine. Then he sinks down on to the floor again.*)

JIMMY. (*Drily.*) Bravo.

LINDA. (*Puzzled.*) I didn't get it.

DENNIS. Did it take long to compose?

IAN. No, matter of fact I thought of it on the shitter yesterday. (LINDA *looks slightly shocked.* IAN *looks at his empty mug.*) Listen, spicy-chops, if you'd care to shift your well-known arse and pull the sofa out you will discover a bottle of superior red. Some rich sucker brought it and I thought pity to waste it down the throats of this guzzling mob so I kicked it discreetly behind the sofa.

LINDA. (*In a tone of arch-disapproval.*) I brought that.

IAN. Oh . . . oh well . . . cheers. (*Takes the bottle from* LINDA *and stumbles round the room kicking things vaguely.*) Where's the corkscrew? (*Turns to* JIMMY, *impatient.*) Where's the bloody corkscrew?

JIMMY. In the kitchen.

IAN. (*Heads for the door, then changes his mind.*) You open it, will you? I'll only shred the cork into the bottle and bugger it up. And if you can't find the corkscrew, shove it in the bread bin and we'll have it for Sunday nosh.

JIMMY. (*Evenly.*) Hadn't you better ask the owner what she wants done with it?

IAN. What?

LINDA. That's all right, you go ahead and open it if you want it.

IAN. (*Hands* JIMMY *the bottle.*) Yeh, you open it. (JIMMY *takes it and heads for the door.*) And be a love and hurry up, will you? I've got to have something to get rid of the taste of that cheap, nasty vinegar I brought.

(*Exit* JIMMY.)

LINDA. I don't think I tasted that.

IAN. No, you wouldn't have; I drank it all myself.

(*As he moves across the room to flop down on the bed next to* DENNIS.) Are you enjoying yourself, Dennis? Have you had a good time?

DENNIS. I . . . yes, I think so, thanks.

IAN. I feel, Dennis, that you are not a great talker.

DENNIS. (*Uncertain.*) Well . . . it depends.

IAN. (*Pause.*) What's it like at school now?

DENNIS. Same as ever.

IAN. (*Mellow.*) I don't think I've been so drunk as I am now since the last night of my last term.

DENNIS. I remember that night.

IAN. You do? . . . Yes, I suppose you do. (*Silence.*)

LINDA. I cried when I left school.

IAN. (*Coldly.*) Really? . . . (*He looks at* DENNIS.) So did I. (*Re-enter* JIMMY *with the open wine bottle.*) But Jimmy didn't, did you?

JIMMY. Did I what?

IAN. Cry.

JIMMY. Eh?

(IAN *puts on a moron face and they go into an obviously familiar routine.*)

IAN. Eh?

JIMMY. Eh?

IAN and JIMMY. (*Together.*) Wotcherronabaht?

(*Silence.* JIMMY *pours wine. Business as* IAN *insists on his one-half pint mug being filled.* IAN *sniffs elaborately.*)

IAN. Ah, '47! (*Twirls imaginary moustache.*) A sterling year. (*Silence.*) How about a nice orgy, then? (*He beams at the others who smile a little uncomfortably.*) No, seriously, you know. Nothing spectacular or . . . or anything, just a nice quiet modest little orgy.

LINDA. I don't really think I'd like that.

IAN. No. No, I don't suppose you would. You'd be a bit of an outsider really, wouldn't you? Besides, (*He gulps mightily at the wine.*) you haven't really got the constitution for an orgy—if you don't mind my saying so.

LINDA. Is he always like this?

JIMMY. No, he's usually quite well-behaved and . . . docile. (*To* IAN.) What's the matter with you tonight? Are you sozzled or something?

IAN. No . . . yeah. I'm drunk. And I'm tired. And I'm broke. (*He looks at* DENNIS.) And I'm shy.

LINDA. Shy?

IAN. Yes. (*Recklessly.*) Dennis is one of the people who always brings out the worst in me that way.

LINDA. Why?

IAN. (*Abruptly.*) Look, I don't want to harp or anything but since it is the early hours of the morning and since the last trains have already left and you two will presumably be staying the night and since there are only two beds I don't see how we can decently avoid having an orgy.

LINDA. (*Decisively.*) Well, *I'm* not staying the night. I've got the car.

IAN. Oh, yes. I forgot the car.

JIMMY. You can stay if you like.

IAN. Oh, no, she can't. Not if she's got the car. Because if she goes home, Dennis can sleep on the sofa and orgies will once again become optional.

LINDA. Well. There's hospitality for you.

IAN. Any time. Well, Dennis, are you . . . (*He breaks off as he notices that* DENNIS *is asleep. He pauses, smiles, grasps* DENNIS' *thigh and shakes.* DENNIS *comes awake with a great jerk.*)

DENNIS. What . . . ?

IAN. I was just going to ask you if you were going to stop the night. Please do. We've got the sofa and you can borrow a pair of my . . . (*He notices suddenly that he hand is still on* DENNIS' *thigh and whips it away hasitly.*) . . . pajamas.

DENNIS. (*A little wildly.*) No . . . no. What's the time?

IAN. One-thirtyish.

DENNIS. Christ, I didn't realize. I'd better go. My mother'll be sitting up waiting. (JIMMY *has sat down on the sofa next to* LINDA *and is holding her hand.*) I didn't realize.

IAN. (*Paternally.*) I think you've been in an alcoholical stupor for the past couple of hours, my lad. You'll have a job getting back, though, you've missed your train.

DENNIS. (*More worked up.*) But, God, my mother'll be waiting.

IAN. Ring her up, then.

DENNIS. (*Miserably.*) I can't ring her up. Not at this time of the morning.

IAN. Why not? Ring her up. Say you just missed the last train, tell her you've got a bed here, she won't mind.

LINDA. (*Suddenly.*) Where do you live, Dennis?

DENNIS. Hampton Wick.

LINDA. (*Offhand.*) Oh, that's O.K. I'll drive you back. (*She beams at* IAN.) All settled?

IAN. (*Morosely, almost stunned.*) Fine . . . fine.

DENNIS. (*Delighted.*) Will you really? That's very kind of you indeed.

LINDA. Mm. (*Silence.*)

JIMMY. Are you going to take me for a drive round the . . . er . . . square, Linda?

LINDA. Yes, all right, just briefly, then I'll be off home.

IAN. Oo, goody, I'll come too.

JIMMY. Two's company. You stay behind and . . . entertain Dennis. (JIMMY *and* LINDA *have got to their feet and are heading for the door. Challenging:*) Won't be long.

IAN. (*Riposte.*) Don't forget the . . . fruit gums. (*Exit* JIMMY *and* LINDA. *There is a long silence.* IAN *appears nervous. Then he speaks in a more sober, rather strained voice.*) Dennis. (DENNIS *is asleep.* IAN *slaps his face gently.*) Wakey wakey.

DENNIS. Mm. What? (*He sits up.*) Where's everybody? Where's . . . what's her name?

Ian. Linda . . . having it off with Jimmy in her car. They won't be long.

Dennis. (*Wide-eyed.*) Oh.

Ian. You've had too much to drink. Do you remember that party at school when some disreputable bastard laced you with drink to fulfill his own sinister purposes and then you went back and spewed on the dormitory floor and got into trouble. Do you remember that?

Dennis. I'd rather not. (*Pause.*) It's good of . . . Linda to take me back.

Ian. Like most people, she probably has designs on you.

Dennis. (*Worrying.*) My mother'll be furious. She'll be sitting up waiting. (*Silence.*)

Ian. Look, I've got an idea there. Why don't you ring her up and say someone promised to take you home and you agreed and they stayed on and on and so you can't help being late? Then she can't blame you.

Dennis. That's an idea, that's a very, very good idea. (*Stands up and closes his eyes to concentrate and focus.* Ian *takes his chin in his hands and slaps him lightly.*)

Ian. Have to sober you up a bit first. The phone is there. (*As* Dennis *is dialing,* Ian *is trying to reach something behind the sofa. He finally manages this and emerges flourishing a bottle of whisky. Meanwhile* Dennis *speaks to his mother.*)

Dennis. Hello . . . Mum? This is Dennis . . . yes . . . yes, I know, yes, look, it was because I, you see, this girl person promised to take me home and so I said thanks because it saved me going by train and she's just . . . (*Pause.*) . . . well, she's just . . . (*He dries up.*)

Ian. Stayed on and on.

Dennis. Stayed on and on and I couldn't do anything about it, could I, but I'll be home soon . . . yes . . . yes. . . . I'm sorry about it . . . mmm . . . bye-bye. (*He puts the phone down and smiles at* Ian *who is brandishing the whisky.*)

IAN. Old Jimmy's got some bloody rich friends. Want some?

DENNIS. Yeah, yeah, all right. (*He giggles.*) Did you pinch that?

IAN. They brought it for us to drink, for Christ's sake. (*He pours two ample measures.*) You . . . you don't want water, do you?

DENNIS. Er . . . no. (*Silence.*)

IAN. I . . . I'm . . . in a way I'm sorry I left school when I did.

DENNIS. Why?

IAN. Oh, I don't know, there were a lot of things I wanted to do that I never got round to doing.

DENNIS. Such as?

IAN. Oh, this and that.

DENNIS. (*A flash of shrewdness.*) Mostly that, eh?

IAN. (*Sadly agreeing.*) Mostly that. (*Silence.* IAN *stares at* DENNIS *and sighs.*)

DENNIS. (*Quietly.*) You look sad.

IAN. I am. I am feeling . . . sad.

DENNIS. Why?

IAN. Because now I see the whole thing in perspective looking back and it's funny and ludicrous, but it's sad too.

DENNIS. (*Beginning to lose interest again.*) What? (*Silence.*)

IAN. Listen, Dennis, I want, I think I want to tell you something. See, it doesn't really matter now because situations have changed and I don't feel like I did, not . . . quite like I did and like I said, it doesn't really matter, but I . . . you see . . . oh, shit. (*He takes a gulp of whisky.*) I can't. . . . (DENNIS *is nodding again and* IAN *leans across and squeezes his hand, jerking him back to consciousness.*) See, it's important. I think . . . it's important.

DENNIS. What?

IAN. Well, it was in the summer mostly. . . .

DENNIS. (*Puzzled.*) What are you on about?

IAN. I think you know. I think you knew all the time.

DENNIS. (*Smiles.*) I'm not really with you. Listen, whatever it is, tell it to me straight. Then I'll know.

IAN. O.K., Dennis. Straight. When I . . . (*Another draught of whisky.*) When I was at school I was . . . (*The door bursts open and* JIMMY *stamps in followed by* LINDA. IAN *whips round, angry. After a short silence, poisonous:*) You were quick.

JIMMY. Yes, well, as a matter of fact . . . it's a lovely evening. . . .

LINDA. Morning.

IAN. Is it? Is it now?

JIMMY. Yes, perfect for a walk. Why don't you and Dennis have a walk?

(IAN'S *jaw drops.* LINDA *giggles.*)

LINDA. Jimmy, darling, you aren't terribly delicate.

IAN. You're damn right he isn't. Do you realize you're corrupting the young and innocent with your filthy ways? What's the matter with the car, then? Street lighting? Policemen on the beat? Was the gear lever proving awkward? You always told me, Jimmy, and I took your word for it as one who knew, that there was nothing like a car for a good copulate.

JIMMY. Shut up.

LINDA. Really.

(*Silence.* DENNIS *is fully awake now, enthralled.*)

IAN. So. You want me and Dennis to go for a little walk.

JIMMY. (*Hard.*) Yes.

LINDA. If you don't mind.

IAN. For how long?

JIMMY. About half an hour.

IAN. (*Amazed.*) Half an hour? Half an hour? What's the matter, you haven't got an anatomical deficiency as well, have you? (*He realizes what he has said and drinks deep.* JIMMY *and* LINDA *look shocked,* DENNIS *hurt and suspicious.* IAN *goes on foolishly.*) Whoops.

JIMMY. You watch your bloody tongue.

IAN. (*Stung by* JIMMY's *fury.*) I like your cheek. I like your bloody cheek. You come in here, you order me on to the streets with this poor half-asleep lad here so that you can have a good time. If you think I'm going to tramp the streets, catch frostbite, get arrested for lewd vagrancy just so's you can have half an hour on the . . . pump and thump . . . you've got another think coming.

LINDA. Jimmy said you wouldn't like being interrupted.

(*Silence.* IAN *is temporarily speechless. When he speaks, he is coldly furious.*)

IAN. Oh, did he? . . . Well, he was right. I mean, I find it difficult enough to talk to your sort at any time of the day or night. But I'm tolerant, I tell myself maybe she comes from a good home, poor thing, I make allowances all the time. But when it comes to you marching in here in the middle of the night, commandeering my bedroom, turning me and my guests out into the street, and . . . and parting your thighs all over the furniture, then—then I draw the line.

LINDA. (*To* JIMMY.) You told me he was bad-tempered. But you never told me he was an . . . utter pig.

IAN. Oh, go home, Fanny Hill. Strap your chastity belt back on and do a dramatic walk-out. And don't forget you're giving Dennis a lift. (*Turns to* DENNIS, *speaks with sudden bitterness.*) And you, love of my life, watch out she doesn't rape you on the way home.

LINDA. I'm going. I'm . . . not staying here. . . .

IAN. (*Falsetto.*) To be insulted.

JIMMY. (*Whispering, white with fury.*) Sod off, you.

LINDA. And I hope you're pleased with yourself.

IAN. Oh, I am. I'm going to give me an Oscar. (LINDA

stalks out, snatching her coat. JIMMY *looks at* IAN *with loathing and hurries out after her. Silence.* IAN, *deep breath:*) Well, you'd better go too, Dennis, or you'll miss your lift.

DENNIS. (*Hoarsely.*) Yes. (*Gets up and moves to the door.* IAN *smiles crookedly at him.*)

IAN. Sorry about the unpleasantness . . . er . . . sorry.

DENNIS. That's all right.

IAN. Mm, well . . . keep in touch.

DENNIS. (*Smiles fleetingly.*) Sure. (*Exit* DENNIS. *The door shuts behind him and* IAN *takes another deep breath.*)

IAN. (*Quietly forlorn.*) Cheers. (*He is alone. He stands, deep in thought for a moment then snorts slightly through his nose.*) Oh, Gawd. (*He pours more whisky, salvages a cigarette from a crumpled, left-over pack, lights it and sits down. He makes a strange noise, something between a sigh and a grunt and looks at the door. It bursts open and he looks away quickly.* JIMMY *stands in the doorway, clearly in a rage.*)

JIMMY. (*With quiet hatred.*) Like she said, I hope you're pleased with yourself.

IAN. (*A little uncertainly.*) Like I said, I am.

JIMMY. Because this time, mate, I think you've gone just too far. (*Silence.*)

IAN. Dennis get his lift?

JIMMY. (*Very slowly.*) Did you hear what I said?

IAN. Not really, old bean. Have a whisky.

JIMMY. I said, this time I think you've gone just too far.

IAN. Do you?

JIMMY. Yes, I do.

IAN. (*Turning to* JIMMY, *as if suddenly bringing attention to bear on this point.*) Oh, you do. Well now, is that because you can't bear to see a lady for whom . . . for which you have so great a regard insulted? Or is it (*His voice hardens.*) because you didn't get your thrash?

JIMMY. (*Through his teeth, pointing at* IAN.) Look, you, just watch it. I've had just about enough from you.

IAN. Oh, come now, Jimmy, you can't honestly say you liked that bird. To you she was just meat.

JIMMY. Listen, if I care to go around with . . . with your grandmother, that's my business. And you've got no call to come and stick your oar in just because you're jealous.

IAN. (*Stung.*) Jealous? Jealous? Listen, I wouldn't look at that bird twice if she stripped down in front of me, because I don't like her, see? (*Short silence.*)

JIMMY. (*Mockingly.*) Because you're queer. (*Silence. Now it is* IAN *who is angry.*)

IAN. Don't give me that. You know bloody well if you had to choose between Linda and Dennis, you'd choose Dennis.

JIMMY. Crap.

IAN. (*Quickly.*) You already have.

JIMMY. Shut up!

IAN. After all, let's get this thing in perspective. It was you who tried to turn Dennis and me out of here. You haven't told us why that was, yet. Was it because you were afraid Dennis and I were getting on too well?

JIMMY. Shut up!

IAN. (*Relentlessly.*) You don't fool anybody, you know, with all your fake virility. All this shaving yourself every other day when there isn't a hair on your face, all this devoted attachment to birds, however crummy they are. It doesn't take me in one bit.

JIMMY. (*Almost hysterical.*) SHUT UP!

IAN. (*A climax of pain, anger, and self-reproach.*) You shouldn't start arguments you're too stupid to finish! (*By this time his face is thrust right up against* JIMMY's. JIMMY *breaks and attacks him. A long, grunting, vicious equal fight ensues—no punching, but a swaying, fluctuating wrestling match. During this there is silence except once when* IAN *says "I warn you." Finally* IAN *is on his back in the* C. *of the stage, with* JIMMY *sitting on top of him.* Ian *reaches up and grasps* Jimmy's *biceps and twists him off on to his back.* Ian *follows through, lying on top of* Jimmy. *Then suddenly* Ian *kisses him . . . for a moment they are motionless, then* Jimmy *wriggles from under* Ian *and scrambles to his feet.* Ian *remains lying face down.*)

Jimmy. You BASTARD! (*Kicks* Ian.)

Ian. (*From the floor, broken.*) You knew. YOU KNEW! (Jimmy's *face is creased with pain. He moves quickly across to the chest of drawers and, as in Scene One, produces his hold-all, stands looking at it for a moment. Mumbling:*) I'm sorry . . . I was . . . I'm drunk. (Jimmy *drops his holdall, crosses the room.*)

Jimmy. I'll come back and pack, sometime . . . sometime . . . when you're not here. (*Strides out, slamming the door.* Ian *remains motionless for a moment, then rolls over onto his back.*)

Ian. (*Whimpering.*) Oh, Christ.

BLACKOUT

SCENE 4

ANYHOW, KEEP IT IN THE FAMILY

*About a week has passed. The curtain rises on the same
scene, less the party trappings. It is still extremely
untidy and one of the beds is unmade. The door
opens and* IAN *comes in. He hangs his raincoat up
behind the door, takes off his jacket and flings it
on the sofa. As he is wrenching his tie off, he speaks.*

IAN. Welcome home. (*Sits down on the bed and pulls
his shoes off, sniffs one of them experimentally. Then he
starts looking round for something.*) Slippers. (*He finally
discovers then under his bed, puts them on.*) Supper.
(*Opens the chest-of-drawers and produces one tin of
baked beans and one of spaghetti from among the
clothes. He considers them for a moment in agonized
indecision, then produces a penny and tosses it. He
looks at the penny on the back of his hand, then some-
what guiltily turns it over.*) Beans it is. (*He shoves the
spaghetti tin in the chest-of-drawers, sets the beans down
on the table, and pauses a moment, wrapped in thought.*)
Telly. (*Switches it on.*) Bed. (*While the TV is warming
up, he makes the bed in about ten seconds. The TV has
warmed up, but before the vision appears it functions in
sound only. Unctuous voice from TV:*) Ask the next
mother you meet if she uses "Purge." Chances are she
does—because nine out of ten British mothers do. . . .
(*Switching it off with sudden crisp hatred.*) Then why
the fuck are you bothering to advertise it? Eh? (*He
sighs deeply.*) Bloody liars. (*Suddenly he looks miserable
and cornered. He sits down for a brief moment then
stands up again. Thoughtfully:*) Dennis? . . . (*Decisively.*) Dennis. (*He goes over to the phone and reaches*

38

for the receiver, then hesitates. He clears his throat. He swallows. He touches his forehead distractedly, then firmly picks up the receiver. He dials a number. Pause.) Hello. . . . Is that Dennis? . . . Oh, hello, Dennis, this is Ian . . . *Ian* . . . Yes . . . er, yes . . . pleasure, glad you enjoyed it . . . mmm . . . well, on the strength of the subsequent argument Jimmy moved out. Yeah . . . yeah, I couldn't understand it. . . . Anyhow what I wanted to ask you was would you like to come down tomorrow and we could go to the pictures and . . . You can't . . . Oh . . . mm, well, what about coming down Sunday then . . . I see . . . yes . . . oh, it's quite all right . . . maybe next weekend. . . . Yes . . . I'll ring you this time next week, then? . . . O.K. . . . right . . . bye-bye then . . . cheers. (*Puts the phone down, then, desolate:*) Oh, shit. (*Sits down on the sofa, buries his face in his hands. Suddenly the doorbell rings. He looks up, surprised, gets up, goes to the door. He is gone a moment, then returns with* Mrs. Evans. *As he enters he is speaking.*) . . . Not at all, really. I'm delighted to see you. Make yourself at what I laughingly call home.

Mrs. Evans. . . . Well, I . . . (*She sits down. There is an awkward, charged pause.*)

Ian. (*Suddenly.*) Do you use "Purge"?

Mrs. Evans. (*Blinks.*) I don't think I've ever heard of it.

Ian. (*Casually.*) Nine out of ten mothers do.

Mrs. Evans. (*Uncertainly.*) Oh. . . .

Ian. Actually, that was a stupid question.

Mrs. Evans. Why?

Ian. Because you're an exception. (*Silence.*)

Mrs. Evans. Look . . . I . . . (*She breaks off.*) I suppose you must think I'm absolutely mad, er, bursting in like this. (*She pauses, but* Ian *says nothing.*) . . . but, you see, we had a terrific argument at home and Jimmy was being absolutely beastly and I couldn't stand it so I said I was going to the cinema and walked out. (*She smiles uncertainly.*) They looked really surprised when I said that, you should have seen them. . . . Anyhow, when I was in the car and driving towards London, I suddenly thought of you and I thought you were probably lonely all by yourself and . . . I was lonely, and so I thought . . . I'd come and see you. I hope you don't think I'm too . . . stupid—even when I was outside the door just now I didn't know whether I was going to ring the bell or not . . . I nearly didn't.

IAN. I'm very glad you did. (*He smiles.*) Really. You were right about my being lonely. It's hell on my own in London, it really is. (*Silence.*)

MRS. EVANS. I can't understand Jimmy.

IAN. Why?

MRS. EVANS. Well, I mean . . . he's been very difficult this last week, and argumentative. You remember when you were living with us? . . . Well, he's like he was then only twice as bad. And anyhow I can't understand why he left here so suddenly. He won't say a word about it. . . .

IAN. Well . . . we had an argument.

MRS. EVANS. (*Gentle sarcasm.*) I guessed that. (*Pause.*) What about?

IAN. Oh, er . . . an affair of the heart.

MRS. EVANS. Do go on. It sounds fascinating.

IAN. Well, it was really my fault. During that . . . party last week I took exception to one of his girl friends . . . to . . . er . . . his girl friend, that is, and I was very rude to her, and she left, and . . . Jimmy left shortly afterwards. (*Pause.*) I was drunk.

MRS. EVANS. I'm sure you must have had some reason for being rude to her.

IAN. Oh, yes . . . I had a very good reason.

MRS. EVANS. What?

IAN. (*Succinctly.*) Her breath smelt.

MRS. EVANS. (*Uncertain how to take this, giggles slightly.*) Oh. (*Pause.*) You're really no more communicative than Jimmy. (*Laughs.*) Obviously something really unspeakable must have taken place.

IAN. No, the whole thing was rather a mountain out of a molehill. As are all arguments. (*Silence.*)

MRS. EVANS. You're working again, now?

IAN. Yes, yes—with City and Guilds of London. Tying up parcels of examination papers for various schools. They call it "collating."

MRS. EVANS. That's a very grand name.

IAN. It's . . . fascinating work. (*His voice reveals a deep gulf of misery and boredom.*) Fascinating.

MRS. EVANS. (*With quiet sympathy.*) I can imagine.

IAN. (*A sudden outburst.*) I'm sick of it. I'm there . . . clamped all day. And then in the evening I come home to this. From monotony to loneliness. (*Pause.*) Let me tell you about yesterday. Yesterday was an ordinary lousy day and yet somehow it was lived with a certain intensity. All day I worked thinking about the next tea-break, the next rest-period and I passed the time working out how much I'd earned tying up one particular parcel, maybe if the foreman wasn't looking I could slow up and earn one and four just for wrapping up one small parcel, and that was my pleasure. (*Pause.*) And finally it came to knocking-off time, but I wasn't pleased because there were no more tea-breaks to look forward to, just hundreds of anonymous people making me sweat in the tube, and then the loneliness here that made me shiver. And I had toasted cheese and burnt the toast and my finger and I sat here by myself and watched the telly. And they had one of those retrospective programs, you know, you probably saw it, looking back over the last year, one of those programs about the racial problem. And it kind of brought things to a head. (*Pause.*) Did you see it? (MRS. EVANS *shakes her head.*) Well, it showed various bits of film—it showed the Ku Klux Klan, and an Apartheid supporter, and a man who keeps axe-handles in his restaurant to beat up Negroes, and a group of whites beating up blacks with chairs in a sports stadium in America. And I opened the window. And then they showed the worst thing of all. They showed a Negro policeman in the Congo beating a prisoner—another Negro—to death by hitting him on the head with a club. And I just sat here and watched it; and the man who was being hit wasn't struggling, he was just sitting there, too, he just sat and bled and got beaten to death in my living room. And I switched off. I switched him off because I didn't want him dying all over me. And I sat here thinking about it. And then I saw the flies. I just looked up at the ceiling, see, and there were these flies, hundreds of them, hundreds of little green ones that had come in through the open window. They were all up in one corner of the ceiling, hopping and crawling about. And I went on thinking for a bit and watched them. I'd never seen so many before. And then . . . all of a sudden I was angry. I was furious with these bloody little flies and . . . with everything, so I grabbed a pillow and . . . jumped up on the bed and lashed out at them and killed them and went on killing them till I couldn't see any more and my pillowcase was thick with green specks and remains and my knuckles were bruised where I smashed them against the wall and I was satisfied. For the first time in the day, because I'd done something different and achieved something I was . . . satisfied. (*Long pause as* IAN *unwinds. Finally he speaks matter-of-factly.*) So I went to bed.

MRS. EVANS. I . . . (*She looks distressed.*)

IAN. (*Smiling.*) Don't worry, I'm just playing my usual game.

MRS. EVANS. Which is?

IAN. Making people pity me. I'm very good at it. Very subtly I make the little tableau. Ian reaches out for something, any simple little thing. And his hand stretches out until it's almost got there. And then the hobnailed boots of the Divinity march over my fingers.

MRS. EVANS. Do you believe in God?

IAN. Do I what?

MRS. EVANS. Believe in God.

IAN. I . . . don't know. It doesn't bother me much, I prefer not to commit myself.

MRS. EVANS. Don't you ever commit yourself?

IAN. No. (*Pause.*) Yes. Because sometimes I can't help it. (*He hesitates.*) Sex being a case in point.

MRS. EVANS. You aren't indifferent to sex?

IAN. (*Slowly.*) No. . . . I'm very sensitive to sex. (*Dangerous silence.*)

MRS. EVANS. (*Slight gulp.*) Funny to think you must know more about Jimmy than I do.

IAN. Yes . . . I certainly do. (*Rather bitter smile.*) But then I know more about you than Jimmy does.

MRS. EVANS. Yes.

IAN. Funny.

MRS. EVANS. Yes.

(*Silence. IAN gets up and starts poking about aimlessly.*)

IAN. Oh God, I'm sorry it's such a squalid shambles in here.

MRS. EVANS. (*Instinctively.*) It's not . . . anyhow . . . it's my fault for descending on you without warning.

IAN. I really am absolutely hopeless, you know, I can't cook to save my life. I can't even make bacon and eggs properly in the mornings. Actually, it almost suits my purpose.

MRS. EVANS. Why?

IAN. Because I can't really afford to eat breakfast *and* supper.

MRS. EVANS. Oh, Ian. . . .

IAN. No, I can usually get in quite a good lunch at the canteen. What really gets me down is when I've washed up after supper. I have to wash out shirts, and pants and things. God, it's so sordid. I don't know how to describe the feel of the kitchen.

MRS. EVANS. The feel?

IAN. Gungy. That's the word— (*With relish.*) Gunge. The feel of cold washing-up water full of sour lumps, the feel of the table-top gritted with crumbs and sticky marmelade. (*Smiles.*) I was going to have beans tonight.

MRS. EVANS. Shall I cook them for you?

IAN. No, I . . . er . . . don't really feel like them any more.

MRS. EVANS. Are you sure? Oh, Ian, honestly, it sounds so frightful. (IAN *smiles and shakes his head.* MRS. EVANS *makes a sudden impulsive dive for her handbag and brings out some notes. Mumbling:*) Why don't you have a couple of really good meals?

IAN. (*Takes the money from her, takes the handbag, puts it back inside. Smiles.*) You're very sweet.

MRS. EVANS. (*Confusion.*) I . . . are . . . you . . . it's a long time since . . .

IAN. Now I warned you already. Don't be taken in by my poor unfortunate me spiel. I thrive on moaning.

MRS. EVANS. But really I want to help.

IAN. Do I bring out your maternal instincts?

MRS. EVANS. I'm not sure whether they're maternal or what.

IAN. (*Misinterpreting.*) Now, now.

MRS. EVANS. (*Looks puzzled, then, half realizing what he means, rather worried. Silence.*) Why . . . don't I take you out for a meal?

IAN. No, really, thanks all the same, I'm not hungry. I'd just as soon sit and talk—unless you're hungry?

MRS. EVANS. No, no, I'd . . . just as soon sit and talk. (*Silence.*) What are you going to do with your life, Ian?

IAN. I don't know, maybe I . . . hell, I don't know. Live it. It was enough of a grind getting to University without worrying about careers. (*He smiles.*) Maybe I should work in advertising.

MRS. EVANS. Advertising?

IAN. Yeah, I've got a great idea for a bad breath commercial. Great cathedral packed with people, little persecuted man isolated in the cathedral, maybe between the choir stalls. The choir are bellowing out the "Messiah," vindictively, only it goes: (*He sings.*) "Alletosis,

Alletosis, Alletosis." And tears trickle down the little man's face. And he takes off his little hat and turns to the altar and looks at the Cross . . . and there, clutched in ol' J.C.'s right hand, a tube of Fresho tablets . . . or whatever. And he walks up to the altar, a smile breaking through, with the big backing, like at the end of a Biblical epic. It's great, you see—brings in the old religion. It'll go down big in the Home Counties, I tell you. (*He stops and broods a minute.*) Sorry, not very funny.

Mrs. Evans. I thought it was quite funny.

Ian. Yet another example of my bubbling, irrespressible wit. I'm such a bright little personality, you'd think it would turn my head. (*Pause.*) There's one thing that keeps me sane, though.

Mrs. Evans. What's that?

Ian. The grotesque and repeated failures of my love-life. To put it crudely, very few customers seem interested in the wares.

Mrs. Evans. Isn't a few sufficient?

Ian. Well, the point is, the customers that seem interested get a free sample if I approve of them. But they never come back for more. Consequently business is bad.

Mrs. Evans. How old are you?

Ian. Eighteen; what's that got to do with it?

Mrs. Evans. Younger than Jimmy?

Ian. Yeah, I suppose so.

Mrs. Evans. Well, you can't expect to be an experienced . . . man at eighteen, can you?

Ian. Why not? (*Softly.*) Why not? (*Again brash.*) I know I'm ugly but even so . . .

Mrs. Evans. Don't be stupid. You're not ugly. I think you're quite attractive.

Ian. (*Smiles.*) You are nice. (*Pause.*) Even so, that doesn't mean a lot. I mean, I think you're attractive, but . . .

Mrs. Evans. (*Uncertainly.*) Flattery will get you nowhere.

Ian. I don't think it's trying to get me anywhere.

MRS. EVANS. Ian, I think you're too . . . straight-forward.

IAN. You're so right; I prefer to say honest. I like to think honesty is my premier virtue. Hell, my only virtue.

MRS. EVANS. (*Musing.*) I wonder why Jimmy left you.

IAN. (*Caught off guard.*) What?

MRS. EVANS. Why do you think? Really.

IAN. I . . . told you. We had a great row.

MRS. EVANS. I know, but there must be something else. He's so miserable at home.

IAN. He . . . It's a matter of pride. (*Pause.*) Anyway he's quite welcome to come back. But I suspect we're just not compatible.

MRS. EVANS. Sounds as if you were married.

IAN. (*His self-control regained.*) Well, you started it—asking why he "left" me.

MRS. EVANS. I wish . . . I got on better with Jimmy.

IAN. My mother died when I was twelve. It was funny, we never got on too well. I was atrociously spoilt, a real little bleeder, and I was always having vicious arguments with her about something or other. But I missed her when she went into hospital. They took me to see her on the day she died because she'd been calling for me, and in a kind of delirium. I remember it was a beautiful day in June. She was in a private ward full of sun and flowers—she was quite beautiful, you know. My father was there too. He'd been there all night, he looked all in. They told me not to worry if my mother didn't recognize me. I sat by the bed and held her hand and said "Hello" or something, and she looked at me, and then she said "I'm sorry." She said it two or three times and then I started crying and they took me away. I cried for ages. I couldn't get over her apologizing. There was a person who loved me more than anyone else ever has or ever will—and I didn't realize it until about ten minutes before she—snuffed it. On which note of turgid sentimentality . . .

MRS. EVANS. Oh, Ian . . .

Ian. (*A ghost of a smile.*) That story goes best with the big violin backing. It's always a success with the "Doctor Kildare" fans.

Mrs. Evans. Oh, don't, Ian. Don't be so bitter.

Ian. Oh, great. You be Garbo, I'll be . . . Valentino. (*Drops on one knee; burlesque.*) Bitter? Bitter? How can I help but be bitter when you spurn my love, my love?

Mrs. Evans. (*Puts her hand briefly on* Ian's *head.*) Poor Ian.

Ian. (*Stands up, speaks quietly.*) Pity, I can do without.

Mrs. Evans. (*Hurt.*) I'm sorry.

Ian. (*Smiles.*) My fault. I fish for your pity all evening, and when I get it, I'm annoyed. There's a moral.

Mrs. Evans. What?

Ian. Never give a man what he wants.

Mrs. Evans. That's a bit harsh.

Ian. Yeah.

Mrs. Evans. What do you want?

Ian. (*Softly.*) Experience.

Mrs. Evans. I can't help you there much.

Ian. (*A hint of menace.*) You've got it, I haven't.

Mrs. Evans. (*Out of her depth.*) I know, but . . .

Ian. Yes. Love.

Mrs. Evans. (*Distractedly.*) What?

Ian. Love. Something else. That I want.

Mrs. Evans. Oh. I see.

Ian. Money.

Mrs. Evans. I offered you some of that.

Ian. (*Brief smile.*) Yes, and it's the one thing I can't accept. (*Silence.*)

Mrs. Evans. (*Suddenly.*) Listen. I think I must be going.

Ian. But you've only been here about a quarter of an hour.

Mrs. Evans. (*Breathlessly.*) I know, but . . . I've got quite a long drive and it's about time I was off.

IAN. But you told them you were going to the pictures. That's good for at least three hours.

MRS. EVANS. All the same, I think I must be away.

IAN. Do you want to go? (*A short silence before* MRS. EVANS *answers as she gathers up her handbag and umbrella rather nervously.*)

MRS. EVANS. No, of course I don't *want* to go. . . .

IAN. Then don't go.

MRS. EVANS. I must.

(IAN *looks hurt;* MRS. EVANS *moves over to the door.*)

IAN. It's very lonely, alone.

MRS. EVANS. Go back and live with your grandparents, Ian. I'm sure that would be the best thing.

IAN. (*Slightly petulant.*) I don't want to go and live with my grandparents. I don't like my grandparents.

MRS. EVANS. (*Is confused, agitated. She stands uncertainly by the door, tracing shapes with her umbrella on the floor.*) I don't know what to say.

IAN. (*Smiles.*) Don't worry, I'll rub along. (*Pause.*) Well, it was very nice of you to come, lovely to see you, you cheered me up a lot, and I'm sorry you couldn't have stayed longer. Please come again when and if you can.

MRS. EVANS. I will. (*Silence.*)

IAN. Well, aren't you going to kiss me good night?

MRS. EVANS. (*Hesitates.*) Yes, of course. (*Goes across, kisses him rather clumsily on the cheek, moves away. He stretches out and strokes her cheek gently.*)

IAN. (*Quietly.*) Thank you. Please stay.

MRS. EVANS. I can't . . . I can't. (*Confused smile.*) Good night, Ian.

IAN. (*Sadly.*) Good-bye.

MRS. EVANS. Er . . . good-bye.

(*Exit* MRS. EVANS. IAN *stands quietly for a moment.*)

IAN. (*Sorrowfully, from force of habit.*) Shit. (*Moves around the room, pauses at the mirror, does his hair briefly, notices her lipstick on his cheek and dabs at it half-heartedly. Then he takes the tin of beans from the table and puts it back in the chest-of-drawers. Then he picks up a newspaper, looks in it a moment. He switches on the radio. Second Movement Brahms' String Sextet No. 1.)* Good-oh. (*He stretches out on the sofa. The bell rings.*) Oh, Christ, this is a right visiting day. (*Exit* r. *Pause. Then re-enter with* Mrs. Evans.)

Mrs. Evans. . . . Terribly stupid of me. I'm always leaving them around. Ah, here they are. (*She recovers a pair of gloves.*)

Ian. Well, now you're back, how about a cup of coffee? The kettle's on.

Mrs. Evans. Is it?

Ian. No, actually, but it soon will be. Will you stay?

Mrs. Evans. All right, thank you. (*Sits.* Ian *turns down the radio.*)

Ian. Like the music?

Mrs. Evans. Mm. (*She seems to be thinking about something.* Ian *sits down beside her on the sofa.*)

Ian. Why so pensive?

Mrs. Evans. I don't know. . . . I . . .

Ian. I'm glad you came back. Ian abhors a vacuum. I . . . wish you could be here permanently.

Mrs. Evans. So do I. I'm sorry you're so lonely.

Ian. (*Suddenly drops his face into his hands.*) Oh, God, what am I going to do with myself?

Mrs. Evans. (*Instinctively puts her arm round his shoulders.*) Don't worry, don't. . . .

Ian. (*Keels over slowly till his head is in her lap.*) Help me.

Mrs. Evans. (*Stroking his cheek.*) I will.

Ian. (*Almost imperceptible change of tone.*) Kiss me.

(*Slowly* Mrs. Evans *bends and kisses him on the lips.*)

Mrs. Evans. (*On a rather high note.*) Ian, I . . .

Ian. Again. (*He draws her down and kisses her again.*) Don't say any . . . just . . . no, you're what I need.

MRS. EVANS. No, Ian, I must . . . don't make me.
. . . (*They speak together, broken phrases, almost incoherent. Then a silence. Almost disbelievingly.*) I love you.

IAN. Yes. (*Kisses her again.*)

MRS. EVANS. No. . . . I can't. . . . I can't. . . .

IAN. (*Inexorably.*) Yes.

(MRS. EVANS *submits suddenly, relaxes with a small groan.*)

BLACKOUT

ONCE IS ENOUGH

*About a week later. Saturday night. The room is in the
same untidy state. Enter* IAN *with a large bottle of
beer, which he puts down on the table. He hangs his
coat up behind the door. He stands a moment, thinking, then turns to the mirror and sings to a rhythm-
and-blues tune.*)

IAN.

> I gotta bow-legged woman,
> She got turned-out knees.
> I gotta bow-legged woman,
> She got turned-out knees,
> And my bow-legged woman,
> She gotta stand up when she pees.

And now my piece of advice for the evening. If you
drink, don't stop. (*He turns away, then back to the image
in the mirror.*) You make me puke. (*Opens the beer,
swigs. The TELEPHONE RINGS.*) At this hour of the
night? (*He goes to answer the telephone.*) Hello . . .
oh, hello, Dennis. No, that's all right, I always go to
bed late. . . . Oh, can't you . . . oh . . . I'm sorry
about that. . . . How long is it likely to last? . . . Is
it? . . . Oh, dear. . . . Well, I'm sorry about that, I
was looking forward to it very much. . . . Oh, well,
never mind, maybe some other time. . . . Will you ring
me when you get better? . . . Yes. . . . Sorry you
couldn't make it . . . not your fault. . . . O.K. . . .
Good-bye. (*Slams the phone down with terrific force.*)
Sods. (*Pause, then, resentfully:*) Sounded perfectly
healthy to me. Anyhow, if you've got flu, what are you
doing up at this time of night? (*Pause, miserably.*) You

51

bastard, you've ruined my evening. (*Pause.*) I've been looking forward to you all week. (*The DOORBELL RINGS, making* IAN *jump. He looks surprised and stands for a moment; then thoughtfully:*) I wonder . . . (*Exit* IAN. *He comes back shortly with* MRS. EVANS. *As he enters:*) . . . feeling it might be you, you know. When the bell went, I said, I wonder. (*He smiles.*) I thought it might be you.

MRS. EVANS. (*Uneasy.*) It is . . . me.

IAN. Yes. Well, sit down, make yourself at home, nice to see you. Can I get you something? Coffee? Or would you like some beer?

MRS. EVANS. (*Remains standing.*) No . . . no, thanks.

IAN. Is there something the matter?

MRS. EVANS. No, I . . . (*She sits down suddenly.*) Yes. I had another terrible argument with Jimmy tonight. It was dreadful. He's still idling about the house doing nothing and I said wasn't it about time he thought of doing something, a job or something instead of just mooning about and we . . . set to . . . and it ended up with us having both lost our tempers. I called him a lazy parasite and he called me an interfering old bag.

IAN. Oh, God, what next?

MRS. EVANS. No, it was true in a way, and what I said was true in a way, too. But you know how things get distorted in arguments. It finished up with me bursting into tears and rushing out to the car as before. Silly really.

IAN. People never mean what they say in arguments. Don't worry.

MRS. EVANS. (*Smiles faintly.*) You're quite right. I was stupid.

IAN. No. I think arguments are essential to relationships. They help you see things in perspective. And for my next platitude . . .

MRS. EVANS. (*Smiles.*) I mustn't stay now, my family will be worrying about me if I'm out much longer, it's getting late.

IAN. Mustn't stay? You've only just come.

MRS. EVANS. Yes, I know, but . . .

IAN. You can't go. You've only been here about two minutes. (*Slight change of tone.*) I'm sure you didn't come all this way just to hear me utter a few second-hand words of wiz, did you?

MRS. EVANS. No, I just . . .

IAN. There must be some other reason for your coming, isn't there? (*Silence.*)

MRS. EVANS. (*Almost involutarily.*) Well, I don't want a repeat of last week, if that's what you mean.

IAN. (*A little hurt.*) Oh? Then why did you come?

MRS. EVANS. It would be easier if I left now, I think.

IAN. No, it wouldn't.

MRS. EVANS. What was really in my head was . . . to apologize for last week, but I realize now I'm here that it would be rather . . . inappropriate.

IAN. Apologize? Why apologize?

MRS. EVANS. Because I think I must have been drunk. I behaved disgracefully. It was disgraceful.

IAN. (*Angry now, incredulous.*) Disgraceful? What do you mean, disgraceful?

MRS. EVANS. Well, it was. What I . . . what we did. I would never have dreamed of doing anything like that if I hadn't been drinking.

IAN. Oh, great, that's a new one for the list.

MRS. EVANS. What is? What list?

IAN. The list of excuses people make to me for not wanting to come back for more. That's a right good one— I'd never have let you make love to me if I hadn't been blind drunk.

MRS. EVANS. That's got nothing to do with it.

IAN. Yes, it has. Besides, people always make that excuse and try to exonerate themselves by maintaining they were drunk, when in actual fact they would have done exactly the same if they'd been sober.

MRS. EVANS. That's not true. . . . Look, I came to

apologize to you. And since we're having this out, I think you owe me just as much of an apology as I owe you.

IAN. Oh, do you?

MRS. EVANS. Yes. I wouldn't if you were less mature than you seem to be. But things being as they are . . .

IAN. Oh, the veiled compliment now, is it? Well, I don't think any apologies are due whatsoever. (*Pause.*) And furthermore, limited though my knowledge of sexual matters has been to date, I've found that sex has never been mentioned so specifically in any conversation I've had with any of my partners, unless one or other of us wanted it. And you have driven many miles in the dead of night to tell me that you're sorry we made love last week and you think I should be sorry too. . . .

MRS. EVANS. Yes, I . . .

IAN. (*Inexorably.*) Why did you come?

MRS. EVANS. (*Distraught.*) I've given you my reason already.

IAN. I don't believe it. Why did you come?

MRS. EVANS. (*Breaks at last.*) Oh, for God's sake, shut up. (*Tense silence.*)

IAN. I'm sorry. I don't know what's the matter with me. (*Pours more beer a little uneasily.*)

MRS. EVANS. That's all right. (*Warm smile.*) Well, Ian, perhaps. . . .

IAN. Yeah, yeah, O.K. If you think you ought to. . . .

MRS. EVANS. I'm sorry I came, really.

IAN. No, please don't be sorry; I really am glad to see you.

MRS. EVANS. I won't come again.

IAN. Why?

MRS. EVANS. I don't know. I just think it would be better if I didn't.

IAN. So, as they say, hand on heart, this is good-bye. Come in Mantovani.

MRS. EVANS. I don't want you to be all bitter and twisted about it.

IAN. But I will be. I always am.

Mrs. Evans. Don't make it difficult.

Ian. (*Disgustedly.*) Oh, this is vintage. (*Breaks out.*) I refuse to be affected by sentimentality. (*Covers his eyes with his hand, a brief gesture.*)

Mrs. Evans. (*Pityingly.*) Ian. (*Silence.*)

Ian. (*Wryly.*) Don't forget your gloves this time.

Mrs. Evans. (*Smiles.*) No. (*Stands up.*)

Ian. I shan't forget last week, you know. However many women I make love to in the future, I shall always remember that you were the first. (*Short silence.*)

Mrs. Evans. But I thought you said . . .

Ian. (*Embarrassed slightly.*) No, no, those were different. (*Frosty smile.*) This time last week I was technically a virgin.

Mrs. Evans. I didn't realize. . . . How terrible.

Ian. Terrible? I'm surprised you didn't notice. (*Crooked smile.*) You were very helpful.

Mrs. Evans. Oh, God.

Ian. I shall always be grateful to you. (*Casually.*) Going to kiss me good night?

Mrs. Evans. (*Tries to give Ian a light kiss—but he holds her back and kisses her again. Finally she breaks away from him.*) Stop it! (*Moves away, confused.*)

Ian. (*Murmurs.*) Like mother, like son. (*Louder:*) Why?—

Mrs. Evans. I've already told you. (*Pause.*) Look, you don't seem to realize what all this means to me. I've been married for twenty years now, without ever being unfaithful to my husband. And then, when I met you, I suddenly wanted to be. I can't understand it, I mean, you're nothing special really, are you, let's be honest.

Ian. Oh, charming.

Mrs. Evans. No, Ian, I don't want to offend you, but you're not the most attractive man I've met since I married. Listen, I'm sorry to have to say all this, but I'm trying to understand myself. (*Vehemently.*) I love my husband. Why should I fall in love with a boy of eighteen?

IAN. Don't mind me. Just go right ahead and inter-
rogate yourself and maybe you'll find out what caused
you to suffer such an appalling lapse of taste.

MRS. EVANS. (*With some impatience.*) Oh, don't be
silly. It's all right for you. I've committed adultery, gone
back on twenty years of happy marriage, made myself
feel guilty and miserable . . . for you it was just experience. You didn't take it seriously. It was just the first of
many notches . . . so . . .

IAN. Listen, I don't know about you, but I think it's
very important losing your virginity. I wouldn't waste it
on any old can, you know. It counts for me too, what we
did. Do you think I enjoy breaking up your marriage? I
like your husband a hell of a lot. How do you think I
feel about it?

MRS. EVANS. It's not so important for you.

IAN. I don't count.

MRS. EVANS. It's not so important. . . . Oh, God, I
can't understand why I did it. I'd never do a thing like
that again.

IAN. (*Coldly, almost contemptuously.*) Then why did
you come back for more?

MRS. EVANS. (*Slaps* IAN *hard. Then she collapses into
his arms.*) Because I want you so much. (*Silence.*)

IAN. (*Quietly.*) You're as bad as your son.

MRS. EVANS. What?

IAN. Never mind. (*He looks down at her. Wryly:*)
And now you're had your little catharsis, do you want us
to make love?

MRS. EVANS. (*Amazingly enough with some dignity.*)
Yes.

IAN. (*Pause. He goes over to the window to pull the
curtains, speaks tentatively.*) Perhaps you'd like to get
ready, then. (*Pause.*) Sounds a bit like the dentist,
doesn't it? (MRS. EVANS *begins to unbutton her coat,
slowly.*) Oh, God.

MRS. EVANS. What's the matter?

IAN. Why does it all have to be so sordid? I mean,

I'm not a puritan, at least I don't think I am, but I don't understand why it has to be . . . to seem . . . so sordid. (*Pause.*) Why do we have to make love anyway? Can't you just love me? . . . Isn't there such a thing as . . . Do we have to finish up copulating?

MRS. EVANS. I don't understand you, Ian. We do it because I love you . . . we do it for you. . . . we do it because I thought that's what you wanted. Isn't it?

IAN. (*Shakes his head, bewildered.*) You mean you don't want to?

MRS. EVANS. Of course I do as well. But it's just . . . I don't know. (*Helplessly.*) I told you before I didn't understand it.

IAN. You're just like your son.

MRS. EVANS. (*Suddenly suspicious.*) Why? Why do you keep bringing him into it? I don't know what you're talking about. Why am I just like him, anyway?

IAN. (*Nervously.*) Don't ask me. Don't keep asking me!

MRS. EVANS. I will. You can't just make remarks like that out of the blue. Why am I just like him?

IAN. (*Blurts out.*) Because you don't understand why you're saying yes, and he didn't understand why he said no.

MRS. EVANS. (*After a brief, shocked silence.*) What do you mean?

IAN. You know what I mean. And it's ironical, isn't it? Mm? Salty in the wound. Irony rubbed right right in. (*Shouting.*) Doesn't it make it just about bloody unbearable?

MRS. EVANS. (*Shaking her head; quietly.*) It's not true.

IAN. Why do you think he left?

MRS. EVANS. (*Dazed.*) It's not true.

IAN. (*Blazing suddenly.*) Of course it's true. Do you think I'd have made love to you if I didn't see him in you?

MRS. EVANS. (*Agonized.*) IT'S NOT TRUE!

IAN. IT IS TRUE! (*Sudden, aching silence.*) Oh, God, I'm sorry . . . I . . . (*He stretches out his hand to her.*)

MRS. EVANS. (*Avoiding him.*) Just . . . (*She grabs her coat and handbag and rushes to the door. IAN tries to stop her. She runs out. A long silence.*)

IAN. (*Very quiet.*) We've had this scene before. (*He half-laughs, then crumples onto the sofa.*)

CURTAIN

Scene 6

DOWN THE SNAKE TO SQUARE ONE

About three days later. Evening. Ian *is sitting in chair reading. After a few seconds he flings the book across the room.*

Ian. Crap. (*Sits for a moment, then gets up, goes over to the telephone and lifts the receiver.*) See if this thing's working. (*Dials a number. Pause.*) No . . . no. Bugger. (*Pause.*) Must go in and see someone about this telephone. (*Fishes a biro out of his pocket, reaches for a piece of paper, and writes.*) See . . . about . . . telephone. Oh, I'm too bloody lazy. (*Writes.*) Too . . . bloody . . . lazy. (*Pause. Sighs heavily. Then sings in a heavy American accent.*)

> Oh, mother, tell yo' chillun
> Not to do what I have done,
> Spen' yo' lives in sin an' misery
> In the house of the Risin' Sun.

Dennis; give up Dennis, it's too late. (*Writes.*) Give . . . up . . . Dennis. (*Pause. Inspects himself at length in the mirror, then addresses his reflection.*) You know something, you're going round the twist. (*Shakes his head.*) Must stop talking to myself. (*Writes.*) Stop . . . talking . . . to . . . self. Now what am I going to have . . . ? (*Stops short, glares at his reflection and puts his finger over his lips. Pause.*) No one else to talk to. (*Disgusted by his self-pity, he makes to be playing the violin and sniffing. At this moment the door opens and* Jimmy *appears.* Ian *sees him in the mirror and whips round, taken completely off his guard.*)

Jimmy. I still had my key, so I . . . let myself in.

Ian. (*Nervous smile.*) Well, it's very . . . nice to see you again.

JIMMY. I tried to ring up. I've been trying to . . . ring up quite a few times.

IAN. Yes, the telephone, er, is out of order.

JIMMY. Yes, I know, I told the man yesterday. I said to the operator, er . . . yesterday that I'd rung up quite a few times, so it must be out of order, and he said he'd send somebody down.

IAN. Well, nobody's come. (*Pause. Uneasy laugh.*) British workmen. (*Long, uneasy pause.*) Salt of the earth.

JIMMY. (*Unhappily.*) Mm. (*Pause.*) Well, anyhow, I thought . . . that's what I thought. And so I thought . . . I'd come and see you instead.

IAN. (*Nervous smile.*) Well, it's very nice to see you again.

JIMMY. As your phone was out . . . (*His voice trails away.*)

IAN. (*Concerned.*) Jimmy, what's the matter?

JIMMY. Ian, something terrible has happened.

IAN. What? . . . (*A sense of sudden fear.*) What?

JIMMY. It's my mother. . . .

IAN. What's happened?

JIMMY. (*Pauses, before making a real effort to speak.*) . . . Well, on Saturday, that's last Saturday, Saturday night. (IAN *reacts.*) . . . I expect you were drunk (*Wan smile.*) I expect you'd had a drink or two . . . end of the week . . . (*Long pause.*) anyhow we had a row at home, all of us, although . . . it was principally my mother and me, (*He corrects himself, absurdly.*) I, who were arguing, and, I don't know, you see, I don't know why I got so annoyed, it was so stupid, it was so bloody stupid and petty. (*He smiles to himself.*) She said, one of the things she said, was, why didn't I come back here, and do a job of work like you . . . and I, I said, well, I was pretty angry, I said, if she was so bloody keen, why didn't she come and live with you, and then . . . I can remember it so clearly, you know, the whole argument . . . word for word almost . . . and anyhow, she said

I was no damn good and was a lazy . . . parasite or
something and I called her an interfering old bag . . .
or something, and she . . . well, she was so upset she
just ran out of the house . . . she's done that before,
you know, in fact . . . that was the second time just
recently that she's done that . . . she just runs out and
. . . gets in the car and . . . goes for a drive, I suppose,
till she . . . cools down, and everybody else cools down
. . . and she . . . (*He stops painfully.*) she had . . .
you see, she must have been too upset to know what she
was doing. She had . . . an accident and . . . (*Another
sickening pause.*) she was killed. The car kind of . . .
took off. She was going too fast and she didn't seem
to get to turn . . . this corner. And she went over this
hedge. And that was (*A very long silence.*) . . . it. (*Silence.*)

IAN. I'm sorry, oh, God, I'm sorry.

JIMMY. And it was my fault, Ian. It was all my
fault. . . . (*Pause.*) My fault.

IAN. No, it wasn't. Why should it have been?

JIMMY. Because if I hadn't been such a bastard, she'd
never have gone and got killed.

IAN. No, it wasn't your fault, it wasn't.

JIMMY. (*Quietly.*) Of course it was. (*Silence.* JIMMY
moves across and slumps into a chair.)

IAN. (*Hesitantly.*) Jimmy . . . there's something I
thing I think I ought to tell you.

JIMMY. What?

IAN. (*Silence.* IAN *considers.*) I . . . It doesn't matter.

JIMMY. Yes, it does. What?

IAN. Well, I . . . (*Improvising.*) Well, I was just
going to say, it was pretty fatuous really, but it was wet
on Saturday night, so the roads would have been slippery
anyhow, but it doesn't do you any good to think of that,
anyhow, I shouldn't think, does it?

JIMMY. No. (*Silence.*) She was fond of you, you know.

IAN. (*Wincing.*) I . . .

JIMMY. No, she was, very fond of you. She used to talk about you a lot.

IAN. Well, I was very fond of her . . .

(*Silence.*)

JIMMY. I was going to come back, you know.

IAN. Come back?

JIMMY. Here. I'd made up my mind. I would have asked you to let me come back if this hadn't happened.

IAN. You would have been welcome. Anytime you feel like it.

JIMMY. I can't come back now. I can't leave my father.

IAN. No, of course not. (*Pause.*) I'm surprised you decided to . . .

JIMMY. To come back? Well . . . (*He pauses slightly.*) when I thought about it, I reckoned you were right. As usual.

IAN. (*Looks slightly horrified.*) Right? About what?

JIMMY. Oh, about Linda, and Dennis, and me . . . and us.

(*Dazed silence.*)

IAN. (*Stammering, unaware of what he is saying, almost.*) Linda?

JIMMY. I don't see her any more. (*Silence.*) I don't see why . . . you shouldn't come and stay with us though.

IAN. (*Still dazed.*) Now?

JIMMY. Well, soon.

IAN. No, I couldn't. No, I'd feel like an intruder.

JIMMY. Why, I don't think . . .

IAN. (*Almost without thinking.*) No, I . . . well, I've pretty well decided to go and live with my grandparents.

JIMMY. But I thought you didn't like your grandparents.

Ian. I don't. But I'm sick of living alone. I like myself even less. (*He improvises.*) Anyhow, I've already written the letter to them; I . . . wrote it on Saturday night when I was . . . like you said, a bit drunk and very depressed. (*Silence.* Jimmy *suddenly moves the back of his hand across his eyes. Hastily:*) Er . . . I hope the telephone men come in soon.

Jimmy. (*Struggling.*) They should do.

Ian. Mm . . . I, er, want to get in touch with Dennis before I go.

Jimmy. (*Getting a grip.*) I shouldn't bother, Ian. (*Stands, lets out a short, grunting sigh.*)

Ian. (*Taken aback.*) Why?

Jimmy. (*Embarrassed.*) I don't know. But . . . just take my advice—forget about him. He's not much loss. (*Silence.*)

Ian. This is no time to talk about my lovelife.

Jimmy. (*Surprisingly.*) Coming to see you has been very good for me. (*Smiles, briefly.*)

Ian. How do you mean?

Jimmy. Well, it's taken my mind off . . . things a bit . . . off myself.

Ian. (*Quietly.*) Good.

(*Silence.* Jimmy *sits down again.*)

Jimmy. (*His voice wavering again.*) Talk to me, Ian.

Ian. What about?

Jimmy. Anything. Say anything. Just talk for a bit, so that I'll listen.

Ian. (*Making an effort; after a moment's thought.*) Once, when I was in Paris I went to a lecture. On modern sculpture. (Jimmy *looks up in surprise.*) It wasn't a very good lecture and, as you know, after a time she switched off the lights to show slides, and people started slipping out the swing-doors. And when my eyes got accustomed to the dark, you remember that I looked around and saw I was the only person left in the entire lecture hall.

And I thought to myself, God, I can't go, because if I do, she'll be all alone and lecturing to herself. So I stayed. And about five minutes later she came to an end and switched the lights on and started packing up her things without even looking at the hall. I didn't even have to say anything as I thought I might. I just caught her eye as I was on the way out and smiled vaguely, that was all. And just on an impulse, I hung about a bit outside and watched her come out and she looked perfectly happy, and there was a man waiting for her in a car, her husband I expect, and she got in with him smiling and talking, and they drove off. But when I thought about it afterwards, it seemed to me that it would have been much more . . . satisfying, er, aesthetically or whatever, if I'd left too and she'd been miserable. And so when I came to tell the story, that's the way I told it. (*Silence.*)

JIMMY. And now?

IAN. I don't want to tell the story that way any more. (*Silence.*)

JIMMY. Why did you tell me that?

IAN. (*Smiles.*) First thing that came into my head. I thought you needed distracting.

JIMMY. I did. I do.

IAN. Let's talk about better times.

JIMMY. Last summer. At school.

IAN.

Oh, the forgotten evenings of my youth,
And the remembered afternoons.

JIMMY. (*Surprised.*) Whoever said that?

IAN. (*A short laugh.*) Me. I said it. (*Pause.*) Can't you tell?

JIMMY. Mm. (*He stands up, a little bemused by the odd turn the conversation has taken.*) I reckon I ought to be getting back home now. (*Smiles at* IAN.)

(*Silence.*)

IAN. (*A strange, sharp change of tone.*) It was really all my fault, you know, all this business.

Jimmy. (*Looks at him, worried.*) Why on earth . . .?

Ian. Well . . . well if I hadn't been such a bastard after that party, you'd never have left here, and none . . . of this would ever have happened.

Jimmy. Ah, now, you can't blame yourself because of that. I shouldn't have . . . lost my temper. I mean, anyhow, like I said, what happened didn't really surprise me. . . . (*Embarrassed.*) I mean . . . I half-expected something like that to happen . . . when I moved in. (Ian *gapes at him, stupidly. Silence.*) Well . . . I must be going now. Keep in touch, won't you? And you must come and stay with us sometime, if not just now. (*Smiles at* Ian.)

Ian. Er . . . er, are you sure . . . sure you won't have a drink or something?

Jimmy. No, really, I must be getting home. I just came down to tell you . . . the news. I thought you'd like to know.

Ian. (*Still numb.*) Like? Oh, yes, thank you, it was very kind of you.

Jimmy. (*Stretches out his hand.*) Well . . . cheerio for now, then.

(Ian *takes his hand, they look at each other, then suddenly, spontaneously hug each other.* Ian's *eyes flash for a brief second, then cloud over again.*)

Ian. (*Painfully.*) Sorry.

Jimmy. (*Soothingly.*) Not your fault. (*They separate.* Jimmy *turns and walks to the door, smiles at* Ian.) Thanks.

Ian. (*Wondering.*) What for?

Jimmy. For helping.

(*Exit* Jimmy. *Long silence as* Ian *stares at the doorway.*)

Ian. (*Without moving, his voice full of bitter pain.*)

Always pleased to help people whose mothers I've seduced and killed. (*Silence. Then, with disgust:*) And before long, doubtless I shall be back to go to bed with you. (*Presses his hands over his eyes for a moment, groans softly. Then he drops his hands and goes over to pick up the paper. Empty, hollow.*) What's on the telly?

CURTAIN

PROPERTY LIST

PRE-SET:

Record-player, lying flat. Extreme D.
3 record covers on top of player
Armchair with 1 cushion
TV on top of a coffee table
Ashtray, D. end of TV
2 books U. end of TV
Newspapers and magazines in shelf of coffee table
Open newspaper on floor

Chest of drawers, containing dressing in all drawers except
    the bottom one
Radio D. end of chest
Swing mirror C. back
Ashtray in front of mirror
2 pairs socks
1 alarm clock

CENTER:
Sofa, with 2 cushions, C.
Divan bed (head to o/p.) U. C.
3 cushions on divan
1 pair shoes under the divan
Book case, full of books, lamps set top C.

OFF LEFT:
Coffee table
Open magazine, box of matches, 5 cigarettes, 1 ashtray
Lamp o/p U. corner coffee table
Pile newspapers, magazines, covering phone p/s side of table
Divan bed (head to D.)
Pair slippers, bottle whisky pre-set under divan
Dining table
2 one-half pt., 1 pt. bottle of beer (empty)
1 small Schweppes bottle
1 pt. bottle milk or cardboard udder (empty)
2 mugs
2 glasses, 1 used
1 full bottle lemonade

2 plates with knives and forks, used
One-half a cut loaf
Cigarette packages
Ashtray
Box matches
Record sleeves
Open newspaper

SCENE ONE:

Telephone set under table D. L.
Telephone directories and magazines set on and around
table D. L.
Bed D. L. . . . made up (2 sheets, pillow and cover, magazines,
etc., top end)
Table U. L., two chairs pushed under
On table . . . radio, papers, plates and general rubbish
Bed up R. C. with pillow and cover
Holdall set at R. end
Chest of drawers U. R. . . . mirror on it, and after-shave bottles,
etc.
In top drawers . . . 2 shirts, 2 pullovers, ties, etc.
Dressing in other drawers
TV set D. R.
Couch set C. with cushions
Armchair set off R. C.
Bottles, etc., scattered about
Record player D. of contemporary bookcase
Lemonade set on table

PERSONAL:

IAN:
Wallet and £2.10.0
Watch

JIMMY:
One penny
Wallet and £2.0.0

MRS. EVANS:
Handbag, purse, umbrella and gloves
Collect LINDA's coat for Scene 3
Collect IAN's slippers for Scene 4

SCENE TWO:
Cardboard box set by table U. L.
Duster (IAN)
Dustpan and brush

Off Right:
Tray with 3 cups and saucers, spoons, teapot, sugar bowl, milk jug, plate of biscuits (enough tea in pot for 3 cups only)

SCENE THREE:
Re-set small table
Sofa re-set to face front
Record player set off C. . . . record covers scattered about, party record set on player
Bottles and glasses littered about
Bottle of wine (unopened) and bottle of whiskey set under couch C.
Cigarette packets and ashtrays (full) scattered
LINDA's coat set on U. bed
One-half pint beer mug three-quarters full of red wine (IAN)
Set holdall under bed U.

SCENE FOUR:

Strike:
Cover from U. bed

Re-set:
Sofa

Strike:
Most of party props

Set:
Tin of baked beans and tin of spaghetti on chest of drawers
Slippers under bed D. L.
D. bed unmade
Newspaper set on couch

Check:
MRS. EVANS: purse
IAN: penny

SCENE FIVE:

Set:
Quart bottle of beer on table and several glasses

Check:
Coat with IAN

Re-set:
Chair (D. of table) to face front

Set:
Sofa—straight

SCENE SIX:

Set:
Piece of paper and pencil by telephone D. L.
Newspaper on couch

Re-set:
Sofa
Books on armchair and couch
Chair by U. table
Sofa—to be set

A Man for All Seasons

By ROBERT BOLT

DRAMA—2 ACTS—11 men, 3 women—Unit set

Garlands of awards and critical praise greeted this long-run success in both New York and London. In both productions Paul Scofield was pronounced brilliant for his portrayal of Sir Thomas More in his last years as Lord Chancellor of England during the reign of Henry VIII. When Henry failed to obtain from the Pope a divorce from Catherine of Aragon, in order to marry Anne Boleyn, he rebelled by requiring his subjects to sign an Act of Supremacy making him both spiritual and temporal leader of England. More could not in conscience comply. Neither Thomas Cromwell, nor Cardinal Wolsey nor the King himself could get a commitment from him. He resisted anything heroic; he wanted only to maintain his integrity and belief in silence. But this was treason, and his very silence led him to his death. " 'A Man For All Seasons' is the ageless and inspiring echo of the small voice that calls to us: 'To thine own self be true.' . . . A smashing hit . . . A titanic hit . . . In conception and execution it is a masterpiece."— *N. Y. Journal-American.*

J. B.

By ARCHIBALD MacLEISH

VERSE DRAMA—2 ACTS

12 men, 9 women—Interior

Winner of the Pulitzer Prize for playwriting

The following is from the review of *J. B.* by Brooks Atkinson in the *New York Times:* "Looking around at the wreckage and misery of the modern world, Mr. MacLeish has written a fresh and exalting morality that has great stature. In an inspired performance yesterday evening, it seemed to me one of the memorable works of the century as verse, as drama and as spiritual inquiry. The stage is set . . . in the form of a circus tent . . . Two circus peddlers make whimsical use of the tent by playing God and the Devil. Presently we are deep in the unanswered problems of man's relationship to God in an era of cruel injustices. J. B., a modern business man rich with blessings, is Mr. MacLeish's counterpart of the immortal Job . . . J. B. is brought down by the terrible affliction of our century—deaths and violent catastrophes that seem to have no cause or meaning . . . The glory of Mr. MacLeish's play is that, as in the Book of Job, J. B. does not curse God. When he is reunited with his wife, two humbled but valiant people accept the universe, agree to begin life over again, expecting no justice but unswerving in their devotion to God.

Other Publications for Your Interest

TALKING WITH . . .

(LITTLE THEATRE)

By JANE MARTIN

11 women—Bare stage

Here, at last, is the collection of eleven extraordinary monologues for eleven actresses which had them on their feet cheering at the famed Actors Theatre of Louisville—audiences, critics and, yes, even jaded theatre professionals. The mysteriously pseudonymous Jane Martin is truly a "find", a new writer with a wonderfully idiosyncratic style, whose characters alternately amuse, move and frighten us always, however, speaking to use from the depths of their souls. The characters include a baton twirler who has found God through twirling; a fundamentalist snake handler, an ex-rodeo rider crowded out of the life she has cherished by men in 3-piece suits who want her to dress up "like Minnie damn Mouse in a tutu"; an actress willing to go to any length to get a job; and an old woman who claims she once saw a man with "cerebral walrus" walk into a McDonald's and be healed by a Big Mac. "Eleven female monologues, of which half a dozen verge on brilliance."—London Guardian. "Whoever (Jane Martin) is, she's a writer with an original imagination."—Village Voice. "With Jane Martin, the monologue has taken on a new poetic form, intensive in its method and revelatory in its impact."—Philadelphia Inquirer. "A dramatist with an original voice . . . (these are) tales about enthusiasms that become obsessions, eccentric confessionals that levitate with religious symbolism and gladsome humor."—N.Y. Times. *Talking With . . .* is the 1982 winner of the American Theatre Critics Association Award for Best Regional Play. (#22009)

HAROLD AND MAUDE

(ADVANCED GROUPS—COMEDY)

By COLIN HIGGINS

9 men, 8 women—Various settings

Yes: *the Harold and Maude!* This is a stage adaptation of the wonderful movie about the suicidal 19 year-old boy who finally learns how to truly *live* when he meets up with that delightfully whacky octogenarian, Maude. Harold is the proverbial Poor Little Rich Kid. His alienation has caused him to attempt suicide several times, though these attempts are more cries for attention than actual attempts. His peculiar attachment to Maude, whom he meets at a funeral (a mutual passion), is what saves him—and what captivates us. This new stage version, a hit in France directed by the internationally-renowned Jean-Louis Barrault, will certainly delight both afficionados of the film and new-comers to the story. "Offbeat upbeat comedy."—Christian Science Monitor (#10032)